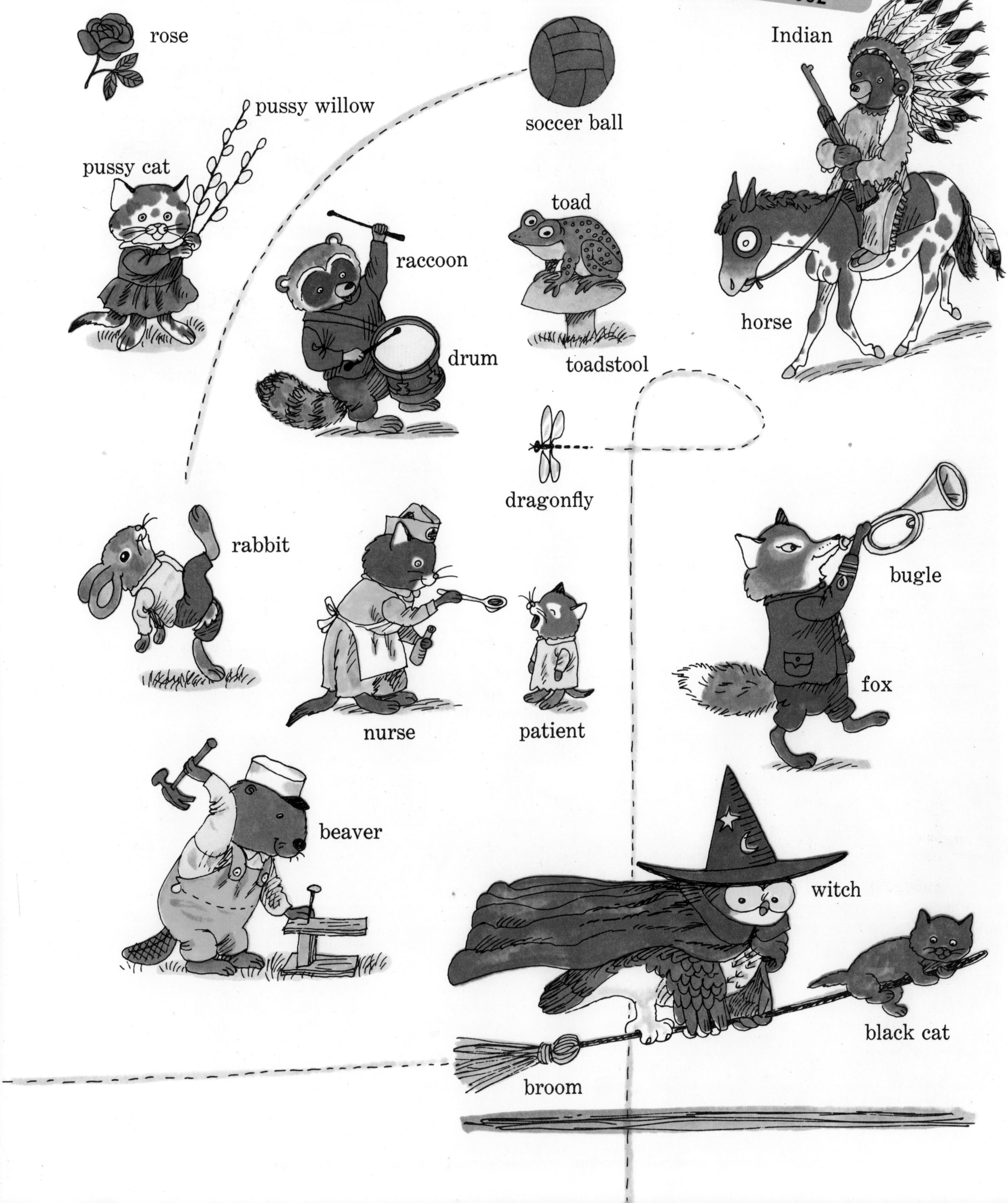
rose
pussy willow
soccer ball
Indian
pussy cat
toad
raccoon
drum
toadstool
horse
dragonfly
rabbit
bugle
nurse
patient
fox
beaver
witch
black cat
broom

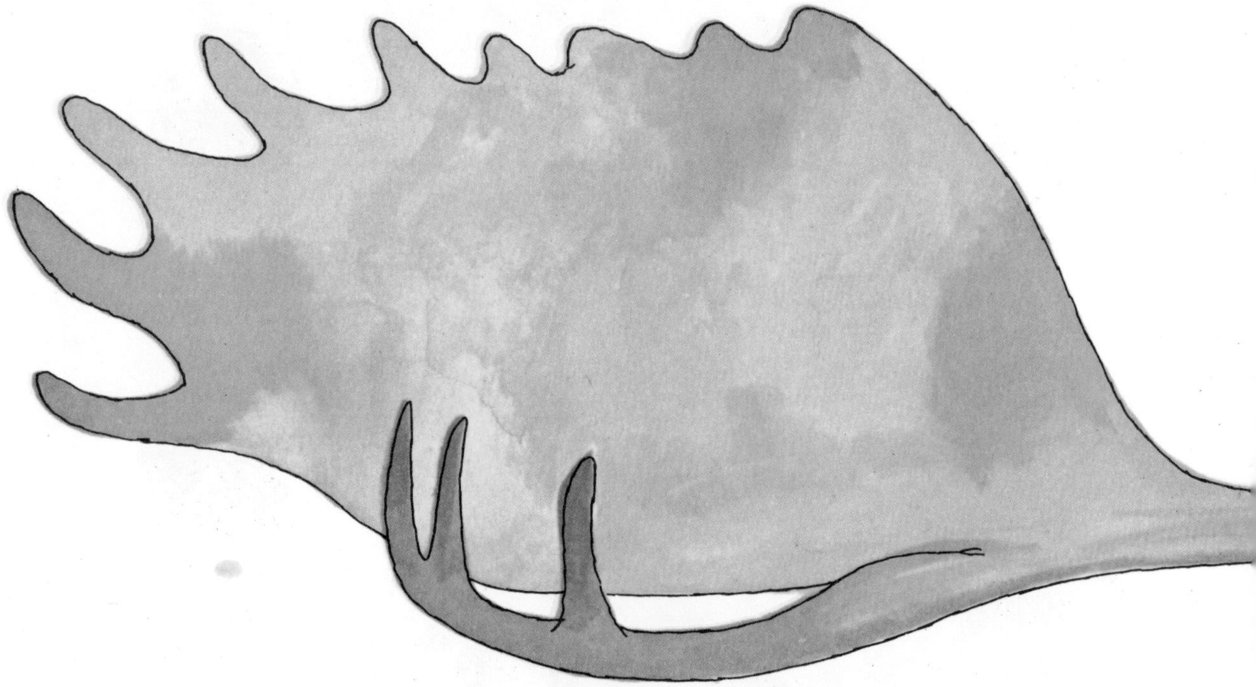

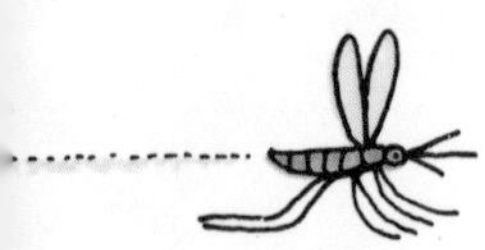

mosquito

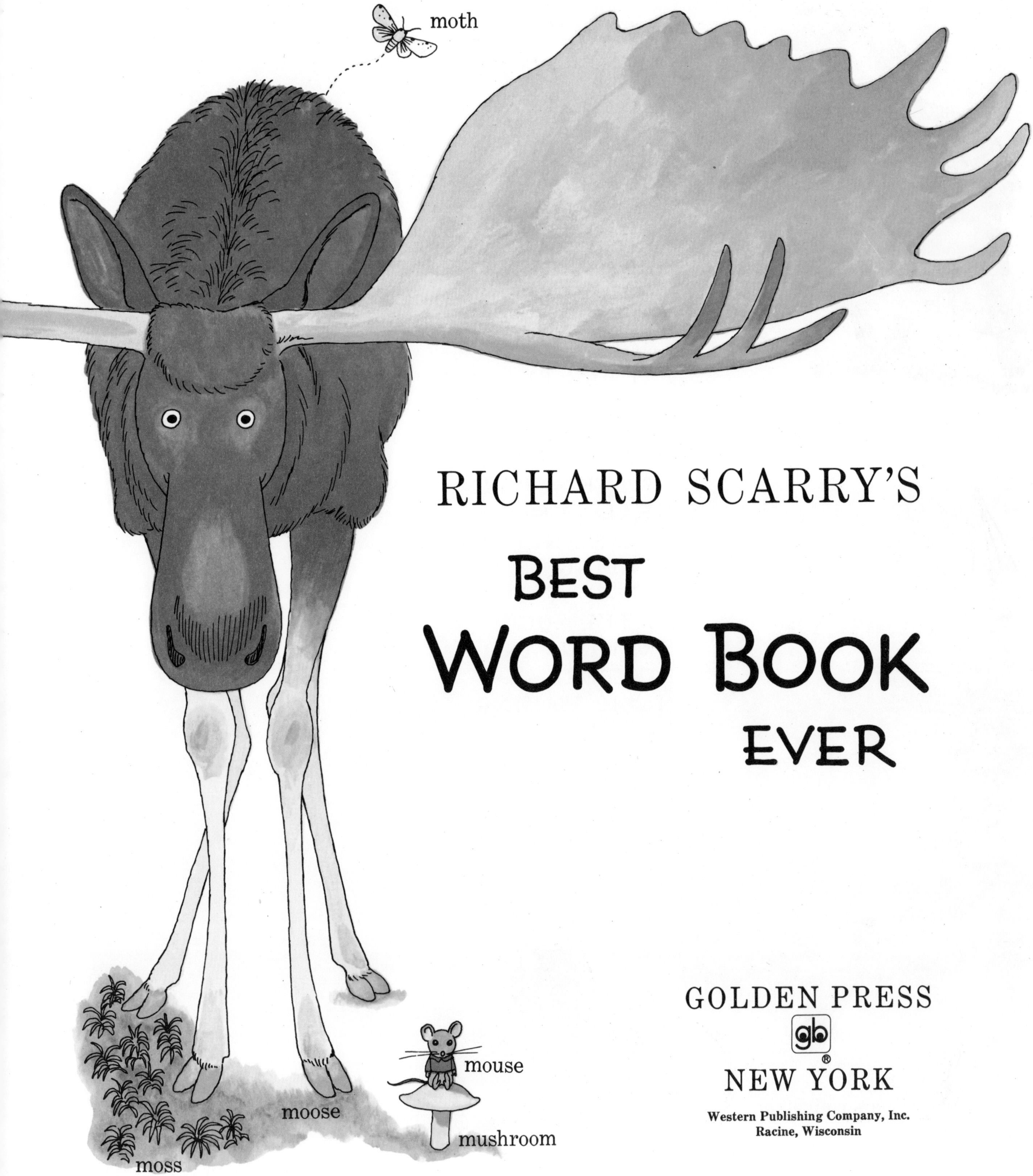

RICHARD SCARRY'S

BEST WORD BOOK EVER

GOLDEN PRESS
NEW YORK
Western Publishing Company, Inc.
Racine, Wisconsin

CONTENTS

THE NEW DAY	8
THE RABBIT FAMILY'S HOUSE	10
AT THE PLAYGROUND	12
TOOLS	14
FARMER BEAR'S FARM	17
AT THE AIRPORT	18
TOYS	20
IN THE FLOWER GARDEN	22
AT THE SUPERMARKET	24
MEALTIME	26
BOATS AND SHIPS	28
KEEPING HEALTHY	30
THE BEAR TWINS GET DRESSED	32
AT THE ZOO	35
DRAWING AND PAINTING	36
NUMBERS	38
MUSIC MAKING	40
IN THE CITY	42
A DRIVE IN THE COUNTRY	44
HOLIDAYS	46
AT SCHOOL	48
IN THE KITCHEN	51

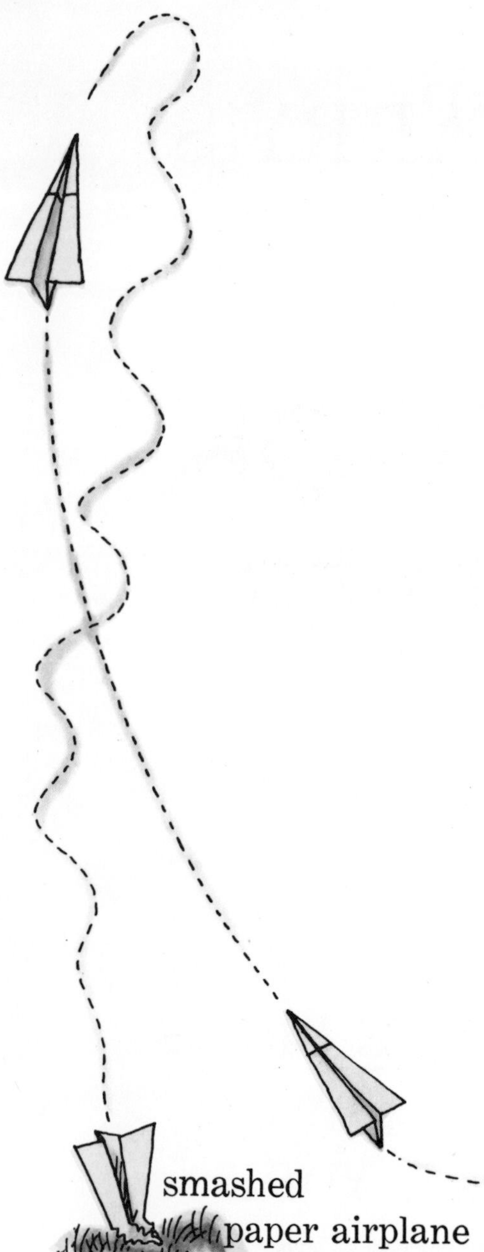

Twenty-sixth Printing, 1979

BUILDINGS 52
WHEN YOU GROW UP 54
THE ALPHABET 56
THINGS WE DO 58
WORK MACHINES 60
CARS AND TRUCKS 63
OUT WEST 65
SHAPES AND SIZES 66
THE BABY 67
AT THE CIRCUS 68
THE FIREMEN TO THE RESCUE 70
TRAINS 72
BIRDS 74
AT THE BEACH 76
HOUSES 78
MAKING THINGS GROW 80
THE WEATHER 81
CLEAN-UP TIME 82
SPRING 84
SUMMER 85
FALL 86
WINTER 87
LITTLE THINGS 88
PARTS OF THE BODY 89
BEDTIME 90
THE LAST WORDS OF THE DAY 92

THE NEW DAY

It is the morning of a new day.
The sun is shining.
Little Bear gets up out of bed.

First he washes his
face and hands.

Then he brushes
his teeth.

He combs his hair.

He dresses himself.

He makes his bed.

He comes promptly
when he is called to
breakfast.

Bear sits up straight
in his chair.

He is very hungry. This is what he
eats.

He doesn't eat
the toaster.

When he finishes eating breakfast he helps his mother to
wash and dry the dishes.

Now he is ready to play with his friends.

THE RABBIT FAMILY'S HOUSE

Father Rabbit, Mother Rabbit, and the Rabbit Brothers are getting ready for the new day. Their friend Owl is waiting for the two brothers to come out to play. Can you find him?

WHOO
owl
smoke
antenna
light switch
television set
record player
hassock
bathroom
upstairs hall
bunk bed
boys' bedroom
front door
living room
outside light
candle
picture
telephone
fireplace
stairs
sofa or couch
front hall
door mat
rug
window
stone walk

AT THE PLAYGROUND

The children are all having fun doing different things. Which children are doing the things you like best?

bubble blowing
kite
jungle gym
merry-go-round
tag
ring toss
hoop rolling
jacks
marbles
sand box
kite string
bouncing ball
hopscotch
4
7
3
6
2
5
8

TOOLS

Everyone is very busy
working with his tools.
Who always carries his
tool with him?
He has a red head.

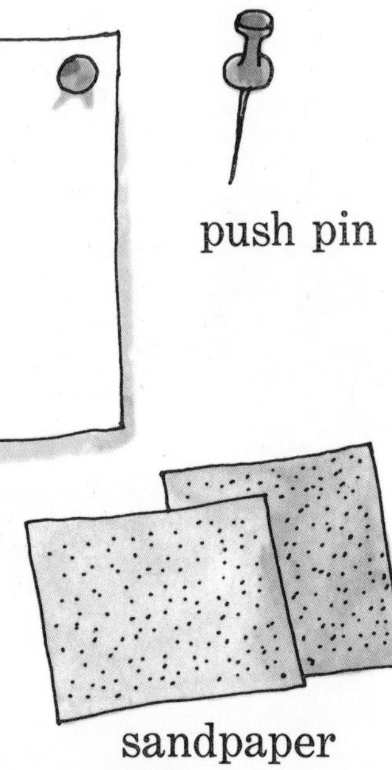

bucksaw
trowel
bricklayer
hoe
brick wall
cement
brick
lumber
fence
painter
paint brush
ball of twine
saw horse
barrel
paint
tack
tack hammer
hatchet
ruler
folding ruler
jackknife
tool box
square
putty knife
shovel
bolt
nut
dirt
monkey
wrench
compass
wheelbarrow
pick axe
glue

crow
scarecrow
weather vane
silo
W
N
E
S
plow
field
tractor
barn
hayloft
goat
tin can
stall
milk can
pail
wagon
hen
rooster
farm truck
pigsty
baby chick
corncrib

FARMER BEAR'S FARM

Farmer Bear has a very busy farm.
What is Mrs. Bear doing? What is the horse doing?
What is the duck doing?
What is the scarecrow
supposed to be doing? He is
not doing it, is he?

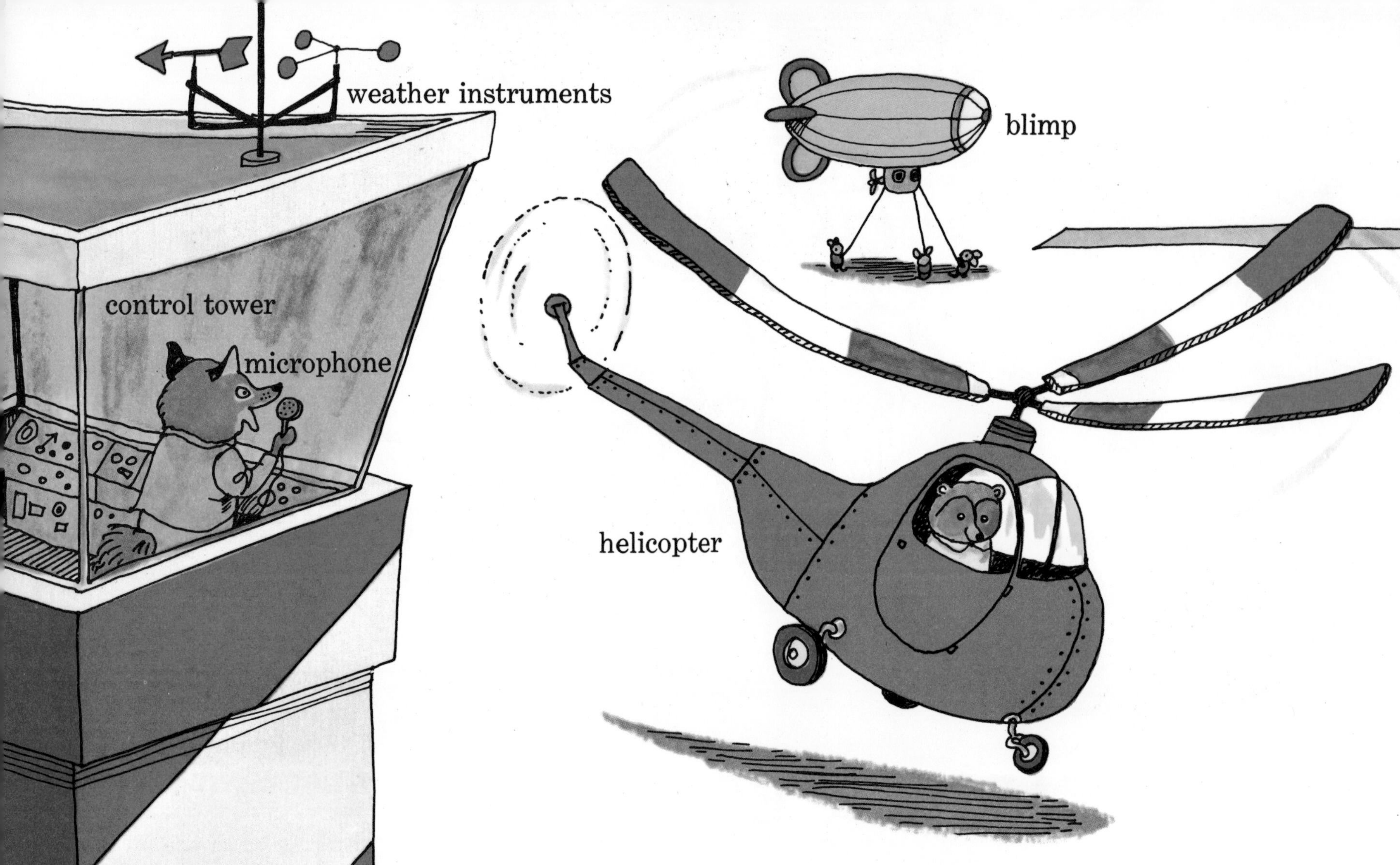

AT THE AIRPORT

The man in the control tower is talking into his microphone. He is talking to the handsome pilot by radio. He is telling him that he will have nice weather on his flight.

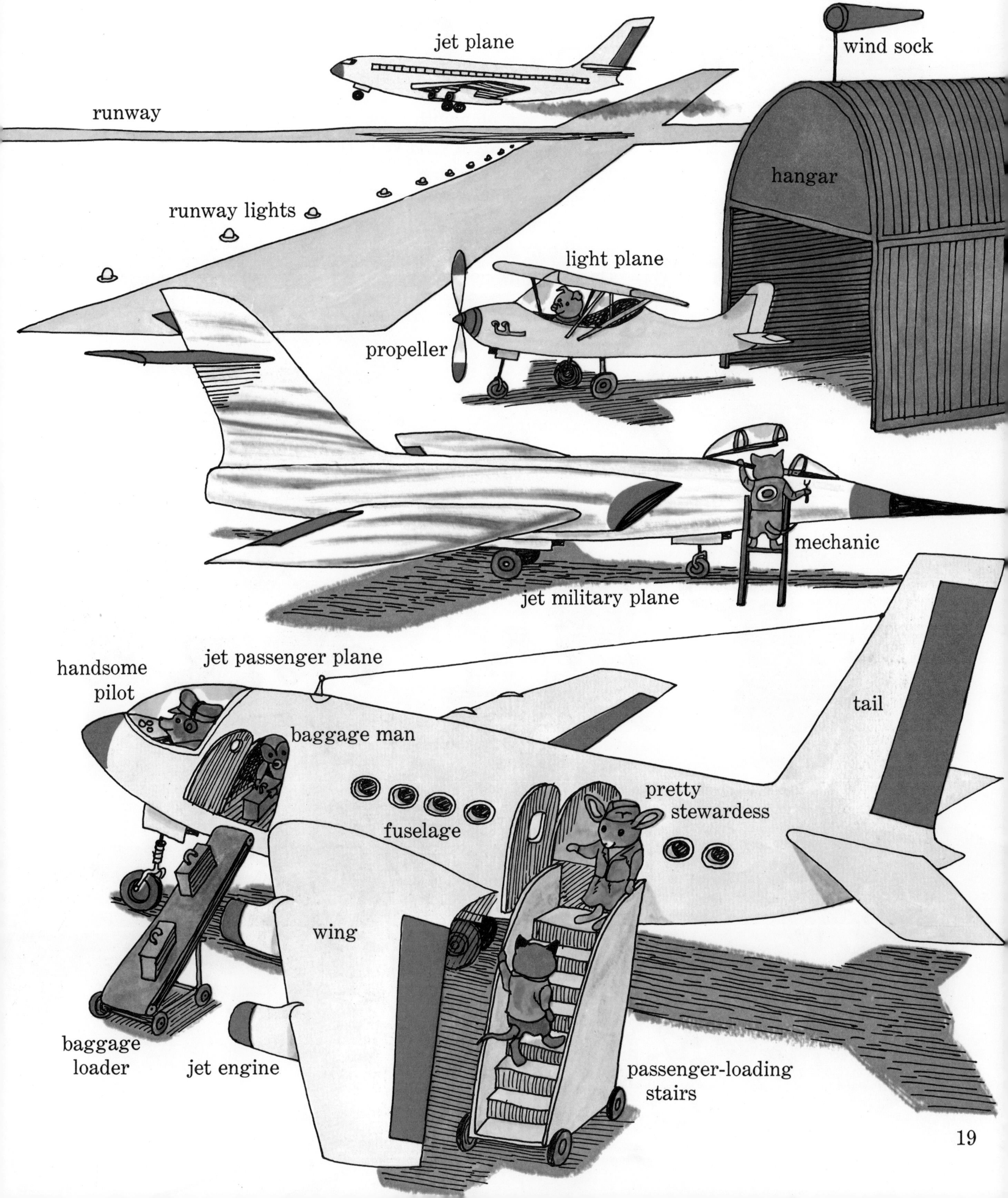
jet plane
wind sock
runway
hangar
runway lights
light plane
propeller
mechanic
jet military plane
handsome
pilot
jet passenger plane
tail
baggage man
pretty
stewardess
fuselage
wing
baggage
loader
jet engine
passenger-loading
stairs

TOYS

When you play with toys, it is more fun if you share them with your friends. When you play games you may win and sometimes you may lose. Bear is a good sport. He is losing a game but he might win the next time. Do you think he might win the next game?

tricycle

electric trains

teddy bear

doll

blocks

truck and loader

Bear is losing.

game

Rabbit is winning.

building set

castle
croquet
toy soldiers
racing car
tea set
robot
typewriter
bean bags
rocking horse
doll house
bow and arrow
glider
scooter

IN THE FLOWER GARDEN

The bunnies love to grow flowers. They spray the flowers to keep the bugs from eating them. They water them to make them grow. Which flower do you like the best?

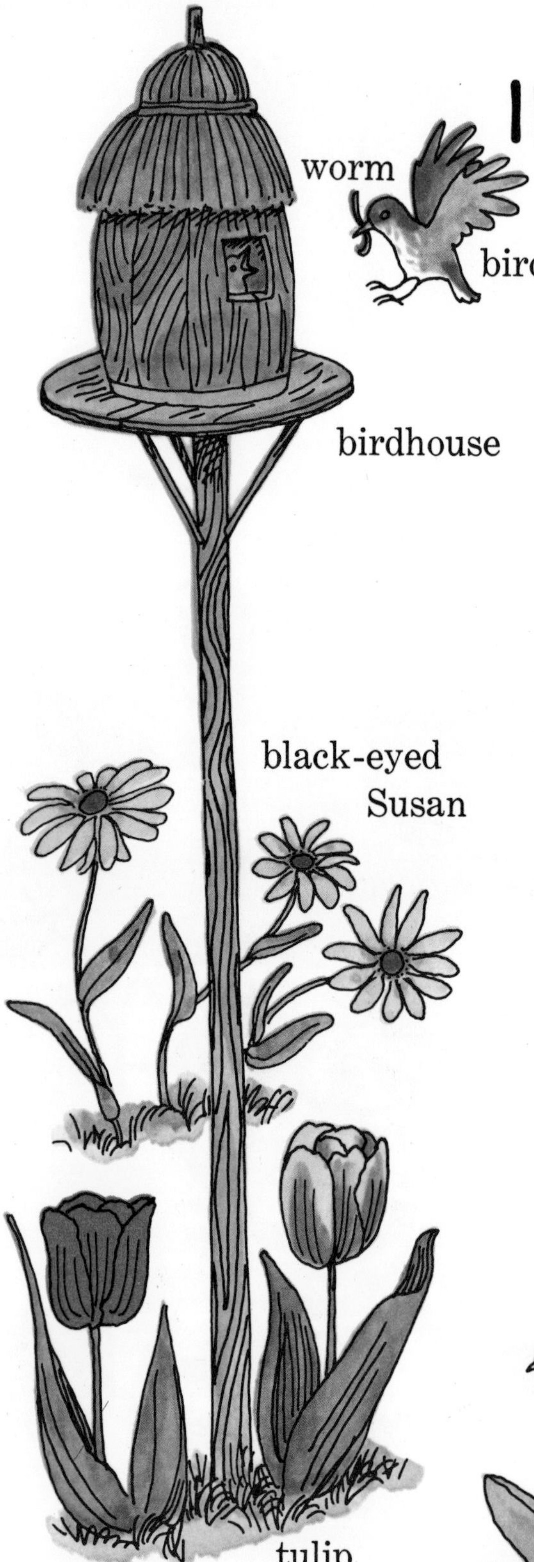

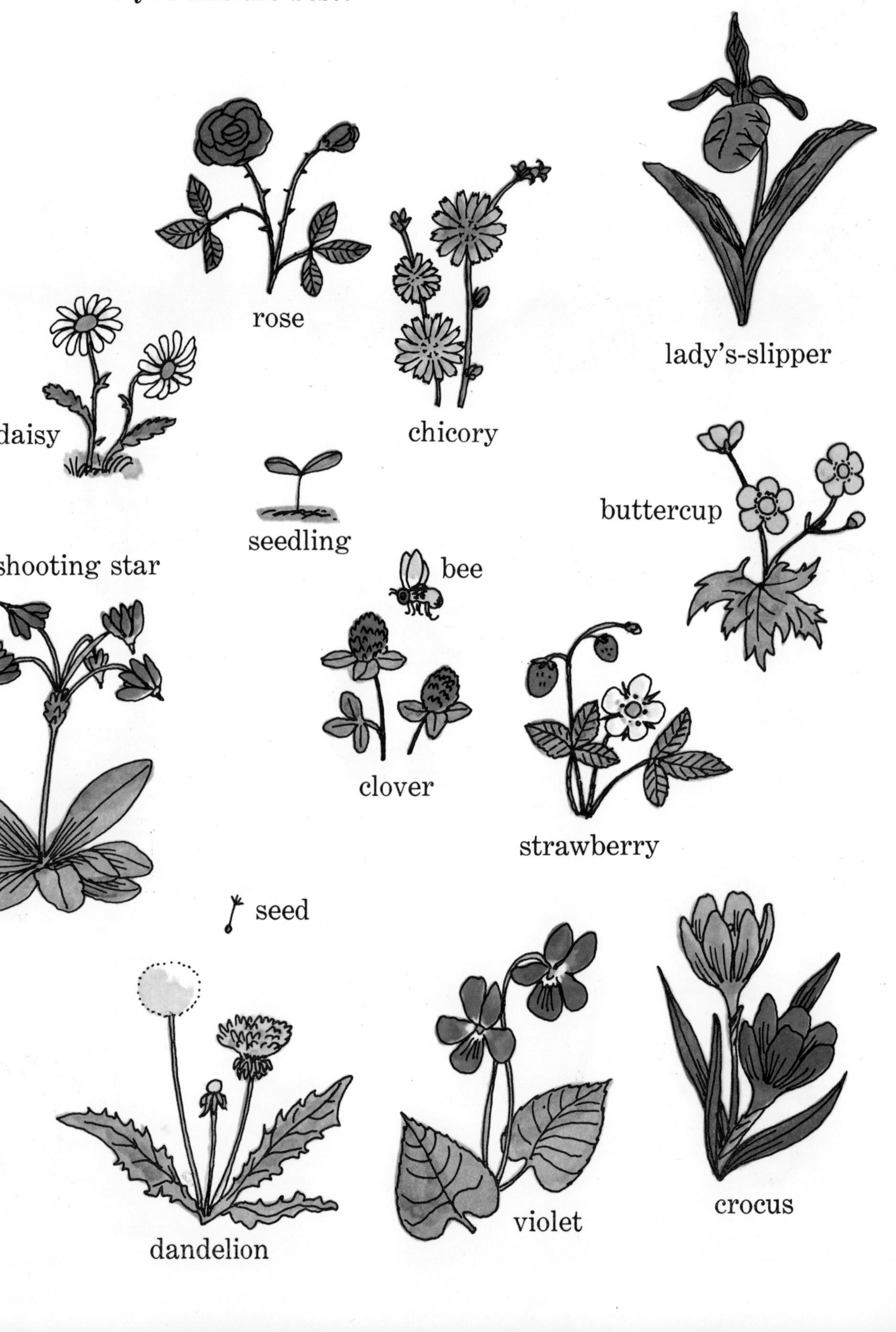

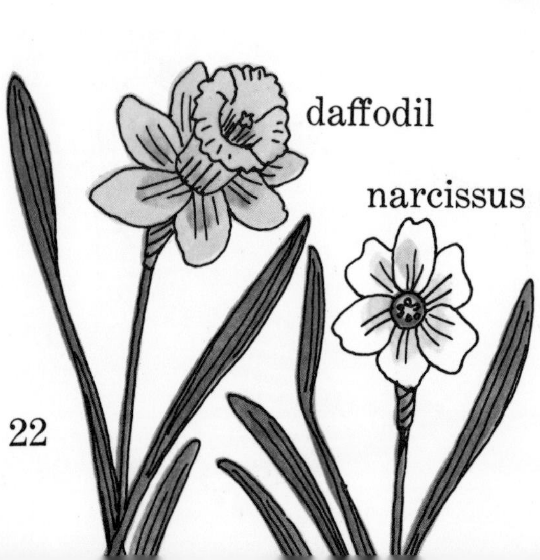

morning-glory
zinnia
hollyhock
sunflower
foxglove
bluet
pink
tiger lily
aster
insect-spray can
bellflower
bluebell
sweet william
petunia
pansy
beetle
poppy
flower basket
seed
watering can
trowel
seed packet
cultivator
lily of the valley
flower pot
bamboo rake

AT THE SUPERMARKET

Mrs. Pig is buying groceries for her family. What would you like to buy the next time you go to the market? Would you like to buy a pickle?

FRUITS
bananas
scales
grocer
pineapple
apples
oranges
pears
grapefruit
melons
grapes
lemons
cherries
strawberries
raspberries
blueberries
plums
0 1 2 3 4 5 6 7 8 9
VEGETABLES
corn
beans
lettuce
tomatoes
peaches
watermelon
pumpkin
asparagus
peas
potatoes
coconut
celery
spinach
cabbage
onions
beets
squash
carrots
cucumbers
cauliflower
turnip
broom
cereal
spaghetti
cookies
sugar
canned food
peanut butter
baby food
cheese
salt
apricots
bread
jam

MEALTIME

Father Pig, Mother Pig, and Peter Pig love to eat. There is so much food on the table it is hard to find Peter.

Can you find him?

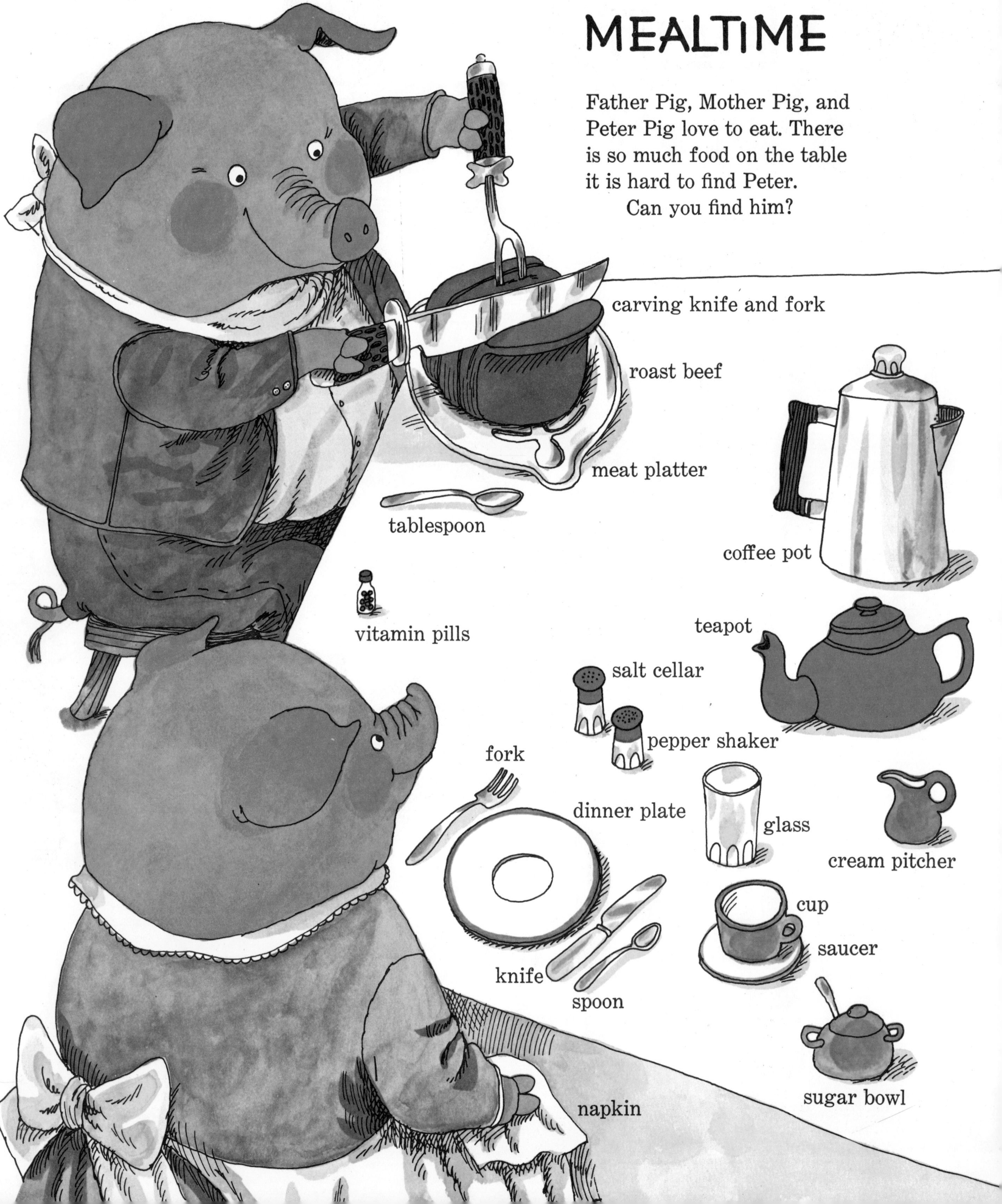

turkey
cake
milk pitcher
squash
baked potatoes
green beans
gelatine
cranberry sauce
mashed potatoes
onions
beets
ice cream
steak
peas
butter
soup
pie
salad
white bread
rye bread
rolls

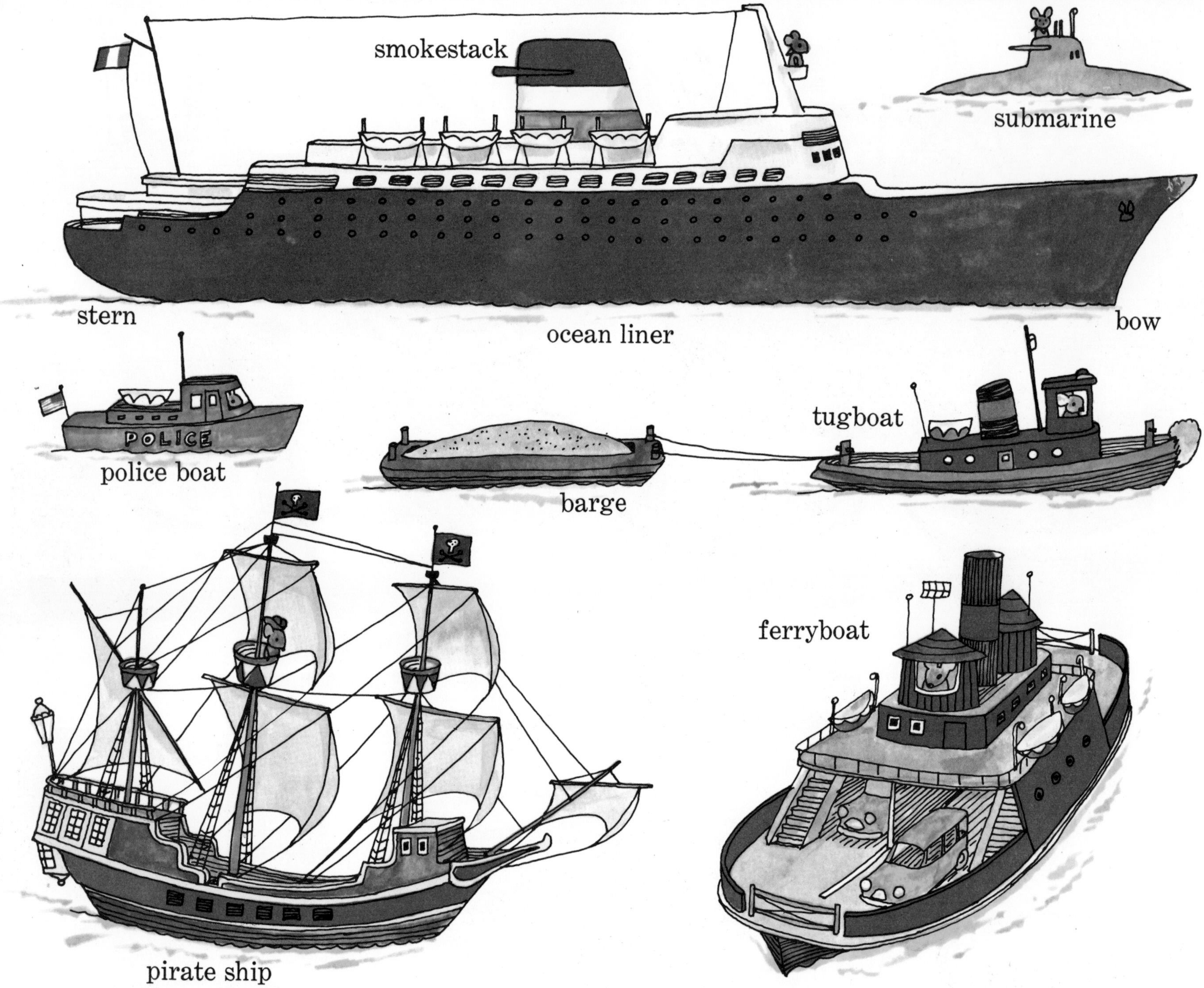

BOATS AND SHIPS

What do you see in the water which is not a boat? It helps boats find the place they want to go.

freighter
lightship
AMBROSE
CG-7
coast-guard ship
oil tanker
F.D.
fireboat
fishing nets
fishing trawler
sport fishing-boat
10
speedboat
houseboat
GRETEL
sailboat
raft
2
lightbuoy

KEEPING HEALTHY

Your doctor and your dentist are two of your very best friends. They want to help you to stay strong, healthy, and happy. Will you give your doctor and dentist a great big smile the next time you see them? How big can you smile?

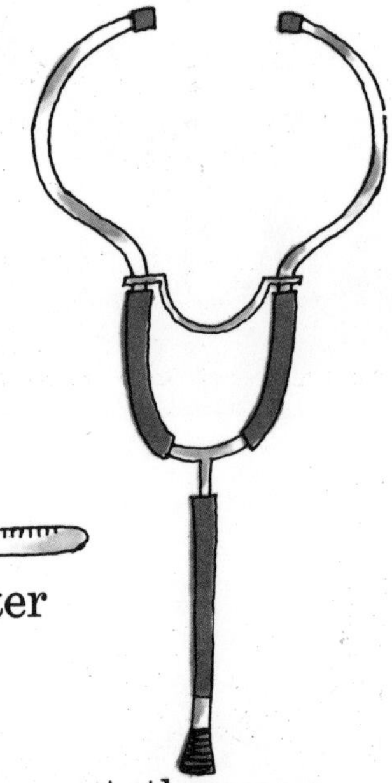

stethoscope

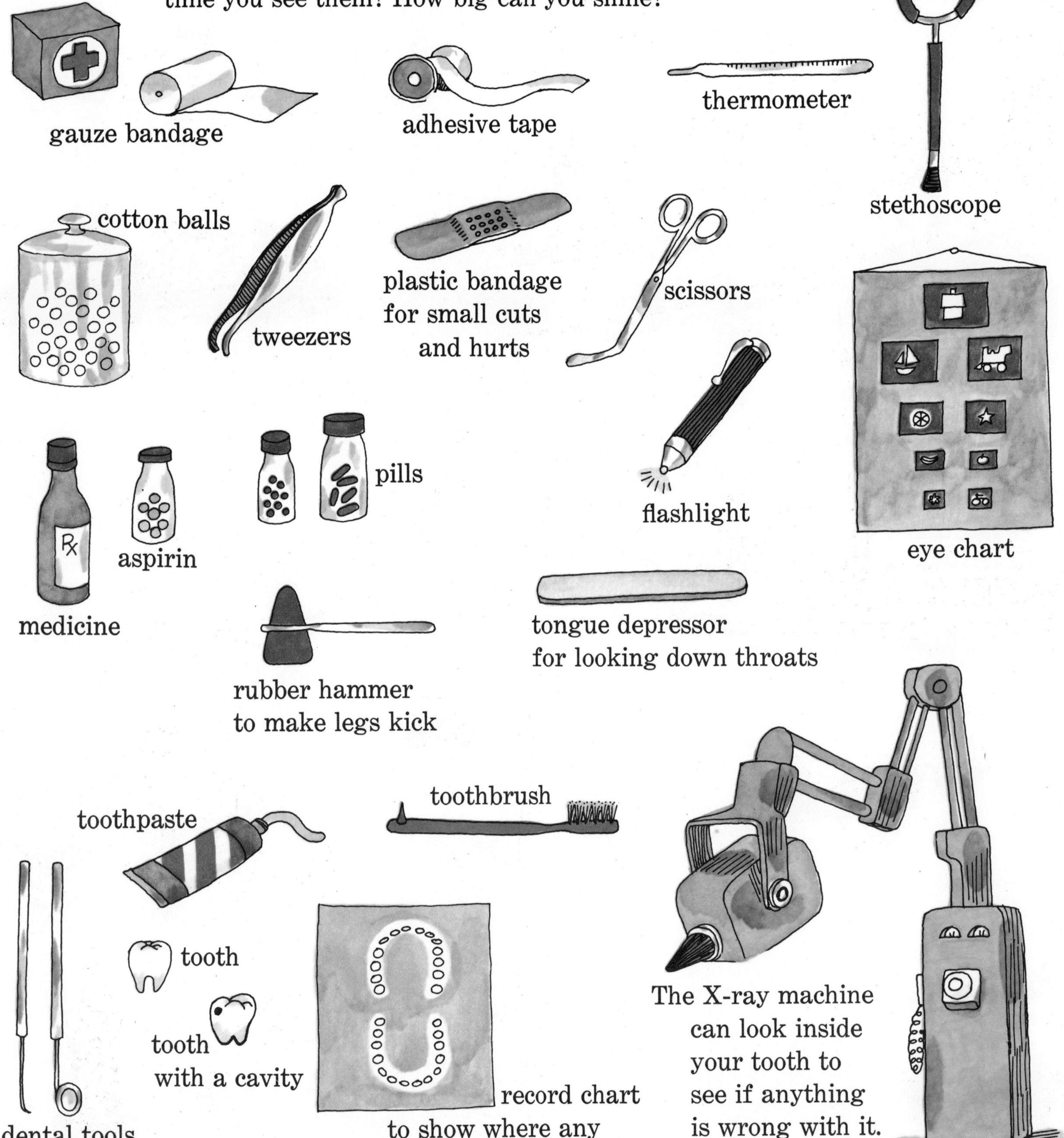

gauze bandage

adhesive tape

thermometer

cotton balls

tweezers

plastic bandage
for small cuts
and hurts

scissors

flashlight

eye chart

medicine

aspirin

pills

rubber hammer
to make legs kick

tongue depressor
for looking down throats

toothpaste

toothbrush

dental tools

tooth

tooth
with a cavity

record chart
to show where any
cavities have been found

The X-ray machine
can look inside
your tooth to
see if anything
is wrong with it.

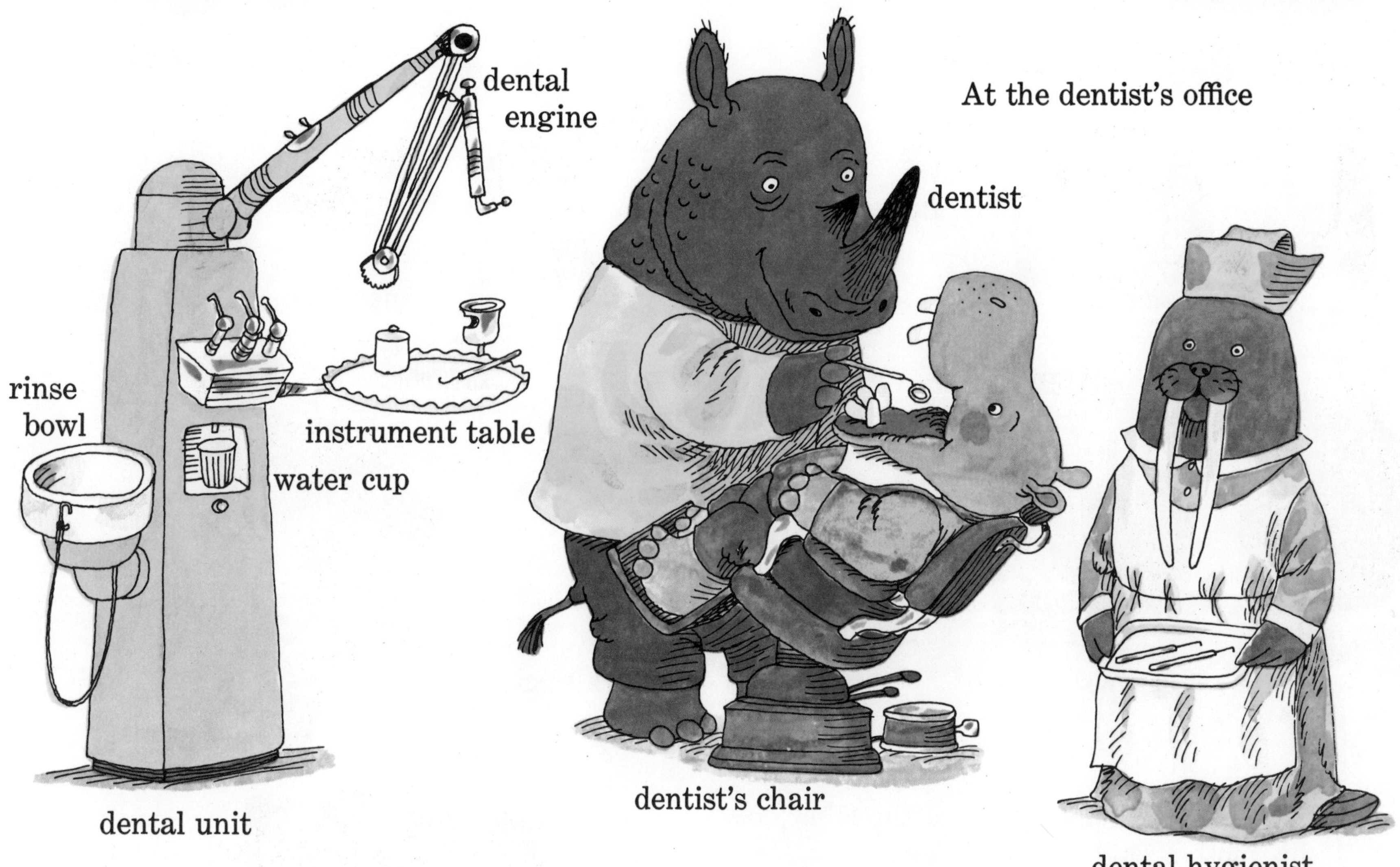

The dental hygienist hasn't a cavity in her teeth.
Brush your teeth well and you may not get any.

THE BEAR TWINS GET DRESSED

Brother Bear awakened one cold, frosty morning.
He wanted to dress very warmly before
he went outside.

He yawned and got up out of bed.

He took off his pajamas
and left them on the floor.
Naughty bear!

slippers

pajama top

pajama bottom

He put on his

underwear

cap

shirt

pants

overalls

necktie

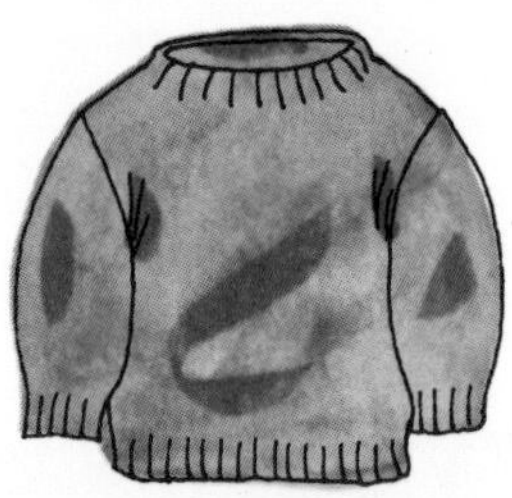

sweater

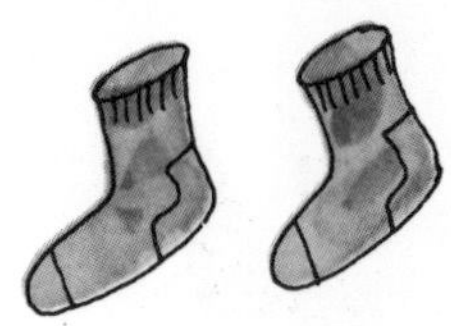

socks

hat

muffler

sneakers

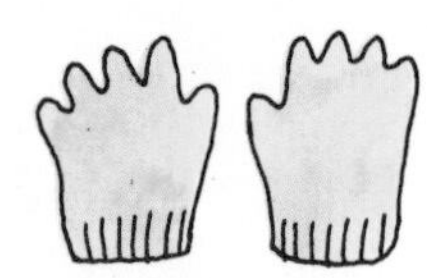

gloves

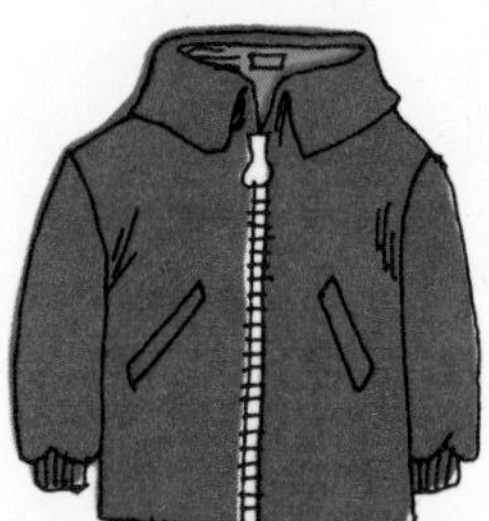

jacket

overcoat

raincoat

and rainhat.

As he was walking out of the front door
his mother said, "Don't forget
to put your boots on!"

boots

Sister Bear got up out of bed.

nightgown

She took off her pretty nightgown
and put it away neatly. Nice bear!

She put on her

panties

petticoat

hair ribbon

blouse

skirt

pinafore

stockings

ear muffs

shoes

snow suit

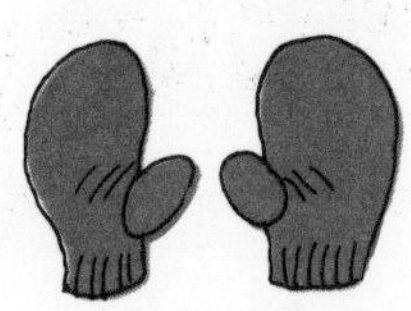

and mittens.

She put her handkerchief

and purse

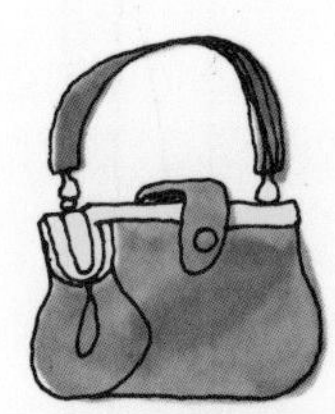

in her pocketbook.

As she was walking out of
the front door her mother said,
"Don't forget to put your boots on!"

Do you ever forget
to put on your boots?

deer
lion
elephant
monkeys
tiger
panda
brown bear
gorilla
polar bear

AT THE ZOO

Mr. and Mrs. Mouse took their children to the zoo. How will those children ever be able to get all those balloons into their house tonight? Which is your favorite animal at the zoo?

DRAWING AND PAINTING

Everyone likes to draw and paint. Can you draw a ferris wheel? They are fun to ride on and they are fun to draw.

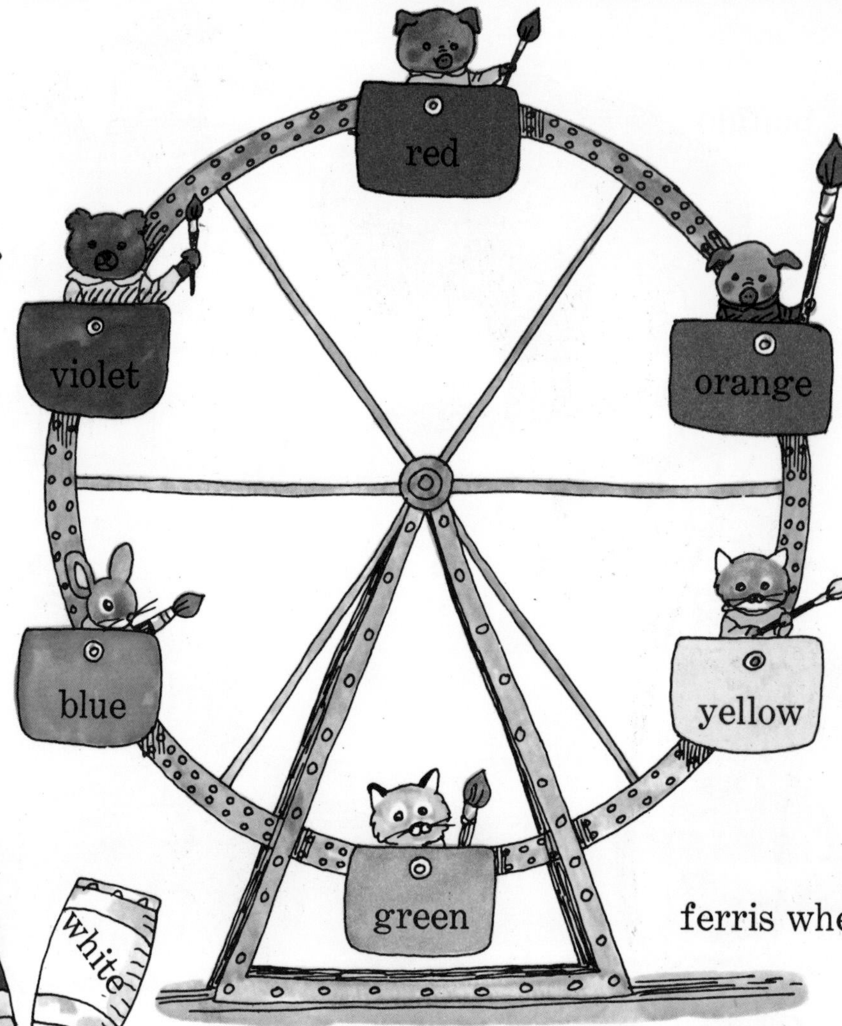

ferris wheel

make orange

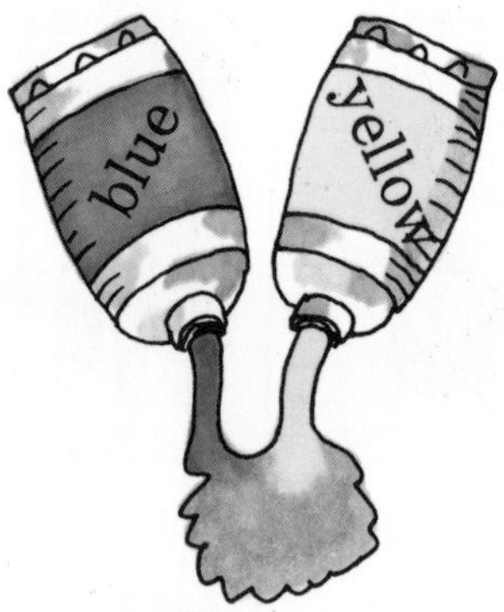

make green

make gray

make violet

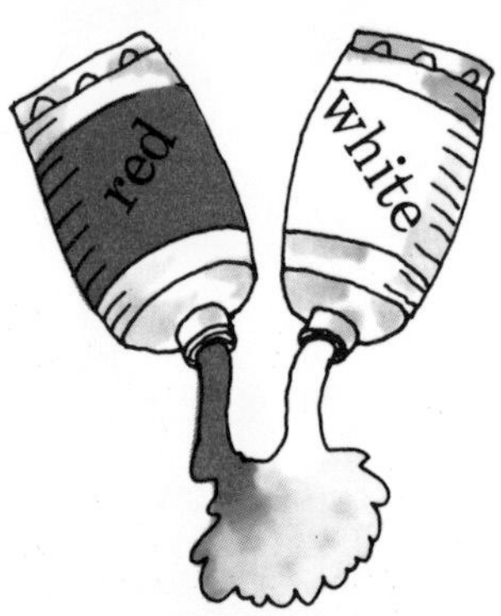

make pink

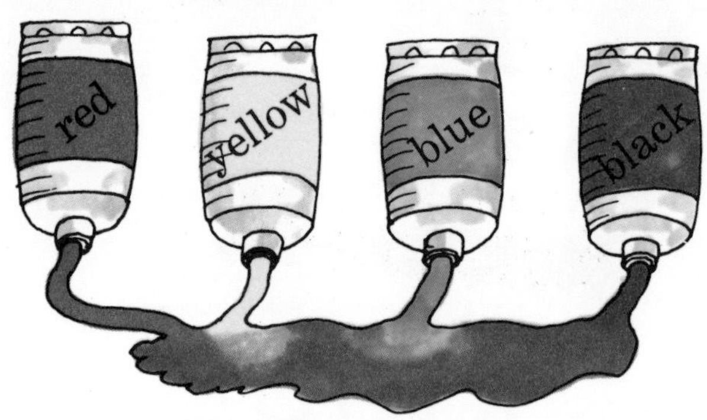

make brown

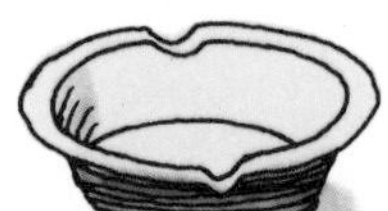

water dish

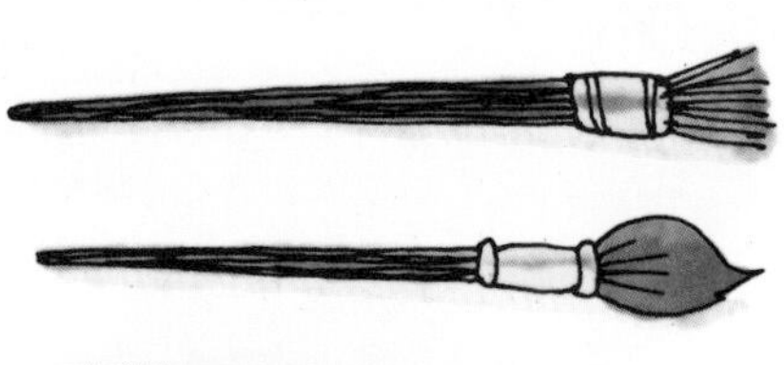

paint brushes

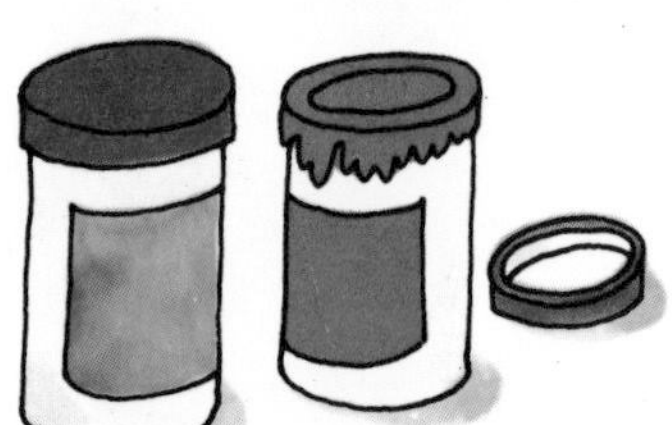

poster paint

eraser

paint box

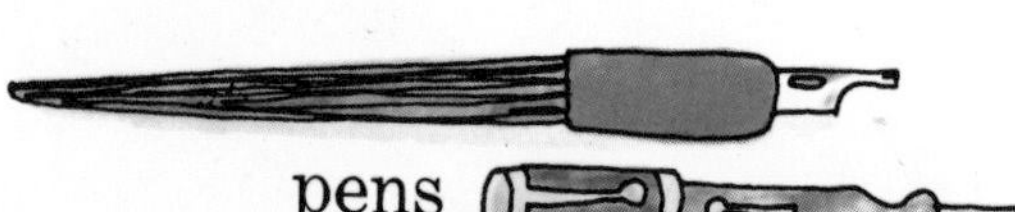

pens

pencil

ink

crayons

pastels

mural painting
artist
dinosaur
scaffold
LIBRARY WEEK
pastel sketch
canvas
still-life model
oil painting
pad of paper
life model
palette
smock
paper
finger painting
watercolor painting
pencil drawing

NUMBERS

How high can you count?
Can you count up to
twenty ladybugs?
I'll bet you can.

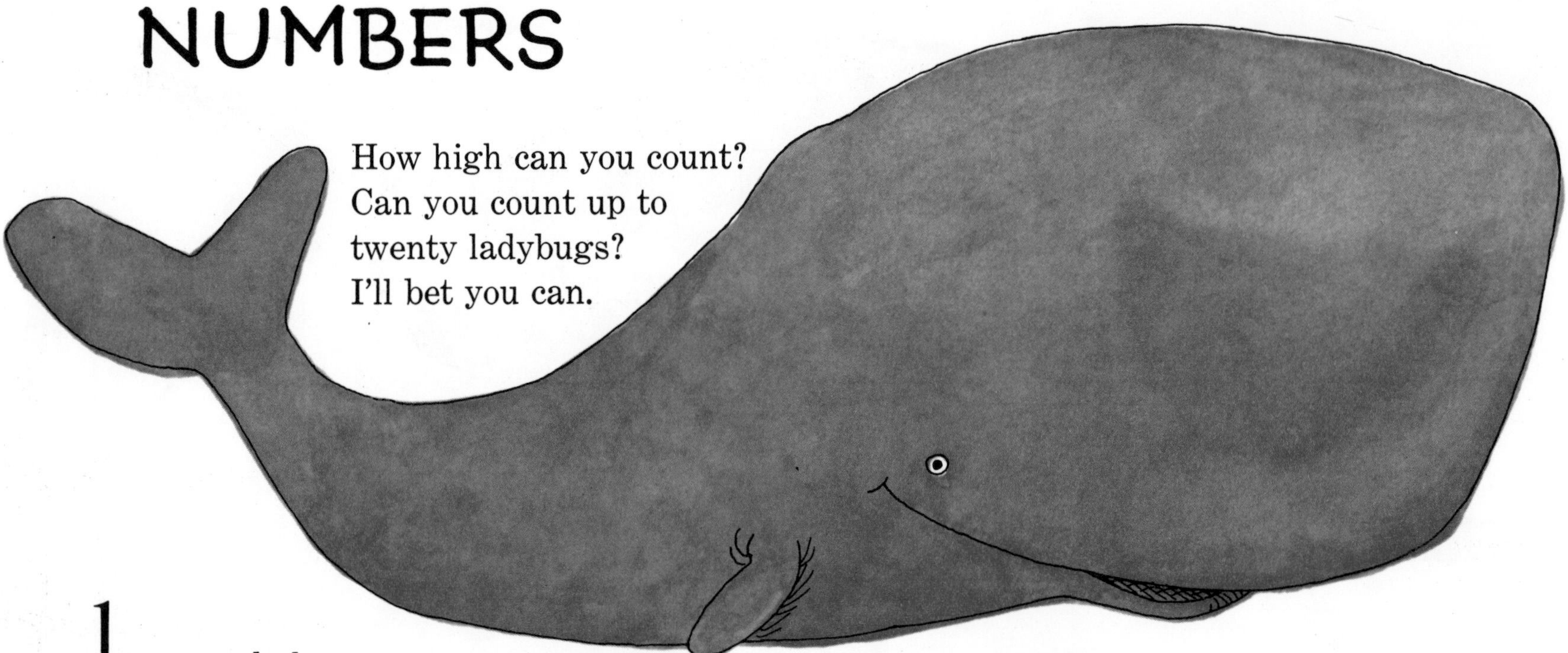

1 one whale

2 two walruses

3 three piggy banks

4 four bells

5 five grasshoppers

6 six eggs

7 seven caterpillars

8 eight spools

9 nine spiders

10 ten keys

11 eleven ants

12 twelve rings

13 thirteen gumdrops

14 fourteen leaves

15 fifteen snowflakes

16 sixteen acorns

17 seventeen pins

18 eighteen buttons

19 nineteen beads

20 twenty ladybugs

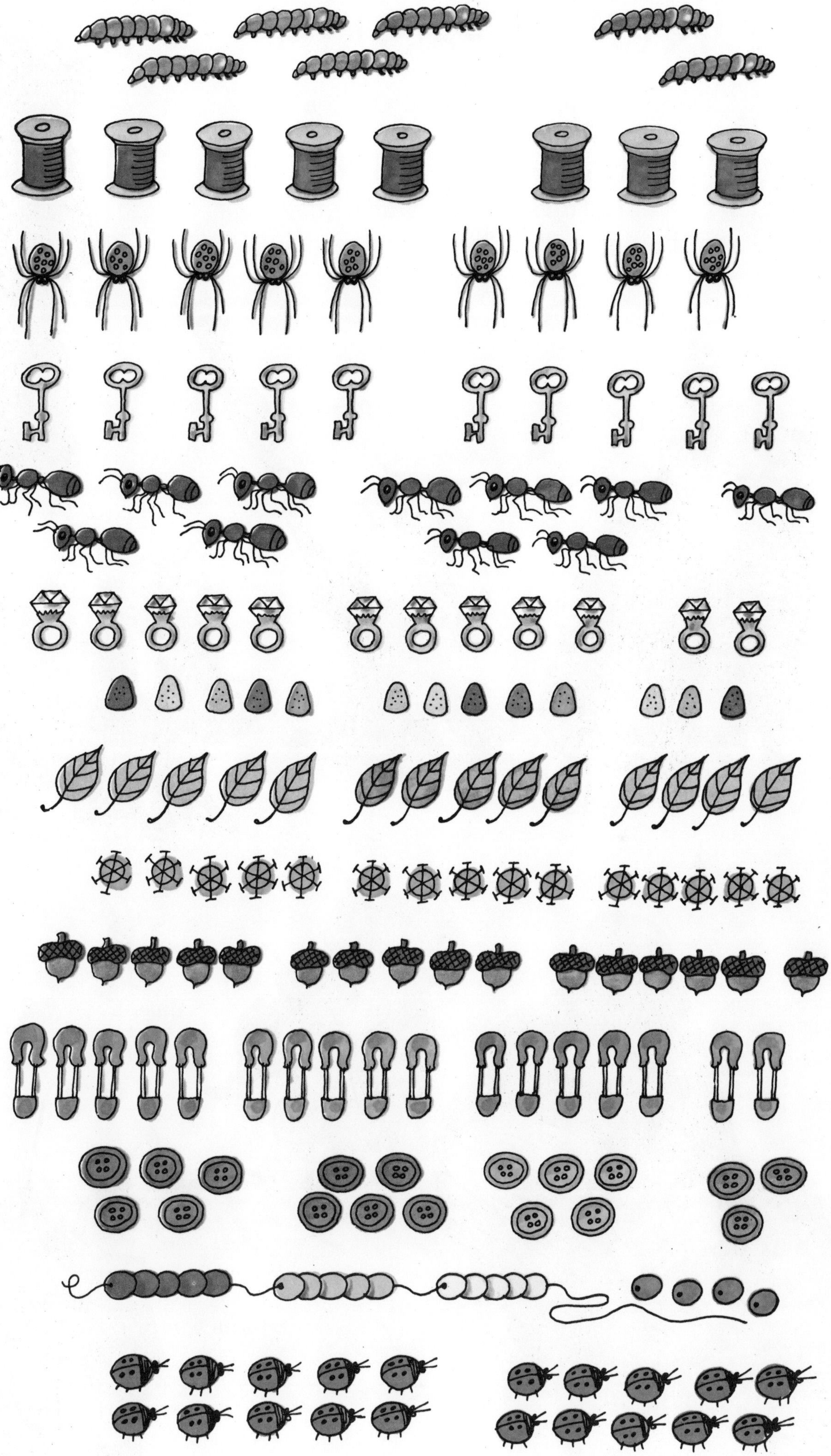

MUSIC MAKING

The conductor leads the orchestra by waving his baton. The musicians are playing a very gay tune. Which of the musical instruments do you think you could learn to play?

kettle drums
snare drum
bass drum
cymbals
triangle
tuba
trumpet
French horn
saxophone
cornet
tambourine
trombone
banjo
guitar
harp
accordion
harmonica
comb and tissue paper

IN THE CITY

Mouse has just bought a book at the book store. He is going to buy a newspaper and then join his rabbit friends at the sidewalk café and drink some lemonade with them. Show with your finger the way he will go. Remember to have him look both ways before he crosses a street.

hotel
street sign
park
park bench
RESTAURANT
statue
manhole
taxi
one way
DANGER
sidewalk café
barber shop
delivery cycle
police car
THEATRE
NOW PLAYING
BUS STOP
TAXI STAND
bus
sidewalk
subway entrance
newspapers
newsstand
subway station

A DRIVE IN THE COUNTRY

There are many things to see when you take a drive in the country. Can you see what the mountain climber has dropped out of his knapsack?

lighthouse
beach
fire lookout tower
crane
bay
drawbridge
woods
seaport
hill
tug
mountain
village
windmill
river
pond
log cabin
mountain
climber
road
forest
knapsack
cliff
apple

HOLIDAYS

Which holiday do you like best? I bet you like them all. Holidays are always very happy times, aren't they? What did you get from Santa Claus last Christmas?

New Year's Day

St. Valentine's Day

Birthday

National Holiday

Halloween

Christmas

AT SCHOOL

pencil

School is fun. There are so many things we learn to do. Little Bear is learning how to find a lost mitten.

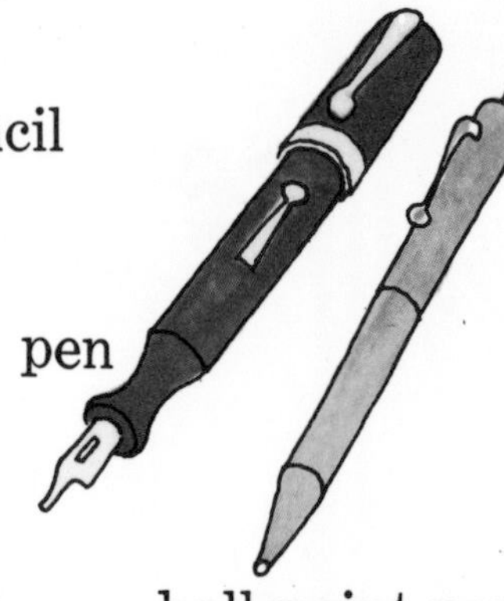
pen

ball-point pen

pencil sharpener

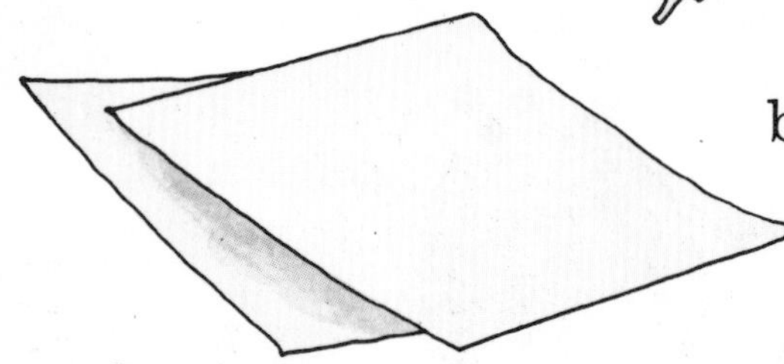
paper

chalk

notebook

straw

milk

ink

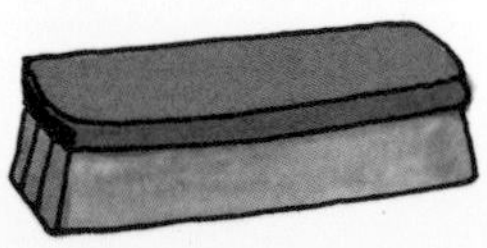
blackboard eraser

eraser

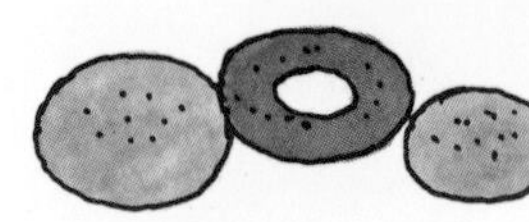
cookies

scissors

string

yarn

paper clip

paste

workbook

storybook

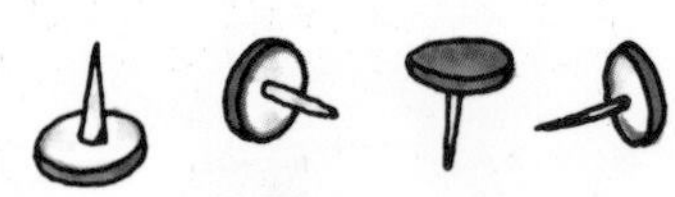
thumb tacks

modelling clay

lost-clothing drawer

flag
clock
bell
blackboard
teacher
calendar
JANUARY
a b c
cat dog
inkwell
map
map stand
waste basket
artist
pupil
desk
classroom
principal
paper dolls

refrigerator
kitchen cabinet
door knob
can opener
soap
teapot
light socket
counter
freezer
garbage pail
clothes-washer
dish-washer
laundry basket
egg beater
egg shell
stool
mixing bowl
batter spoon
measuring pitcher
rolling pin
cookie cutter
dough
strainer
funnel
cake pan
ketchup bottle
cookie tray
spatula
food chopper
flour bin
sugar bowl
mustard jar

IN THE KITCHEN

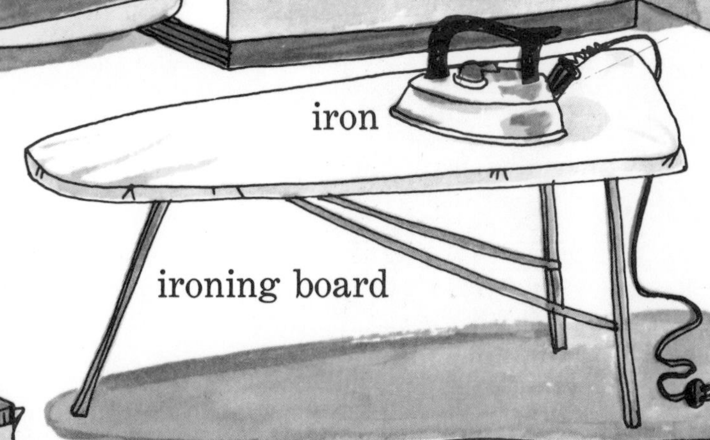

All the little piglets like to help their mother in the kitchen. They are making good things to eat. What is Mother Pig putting into the oven?

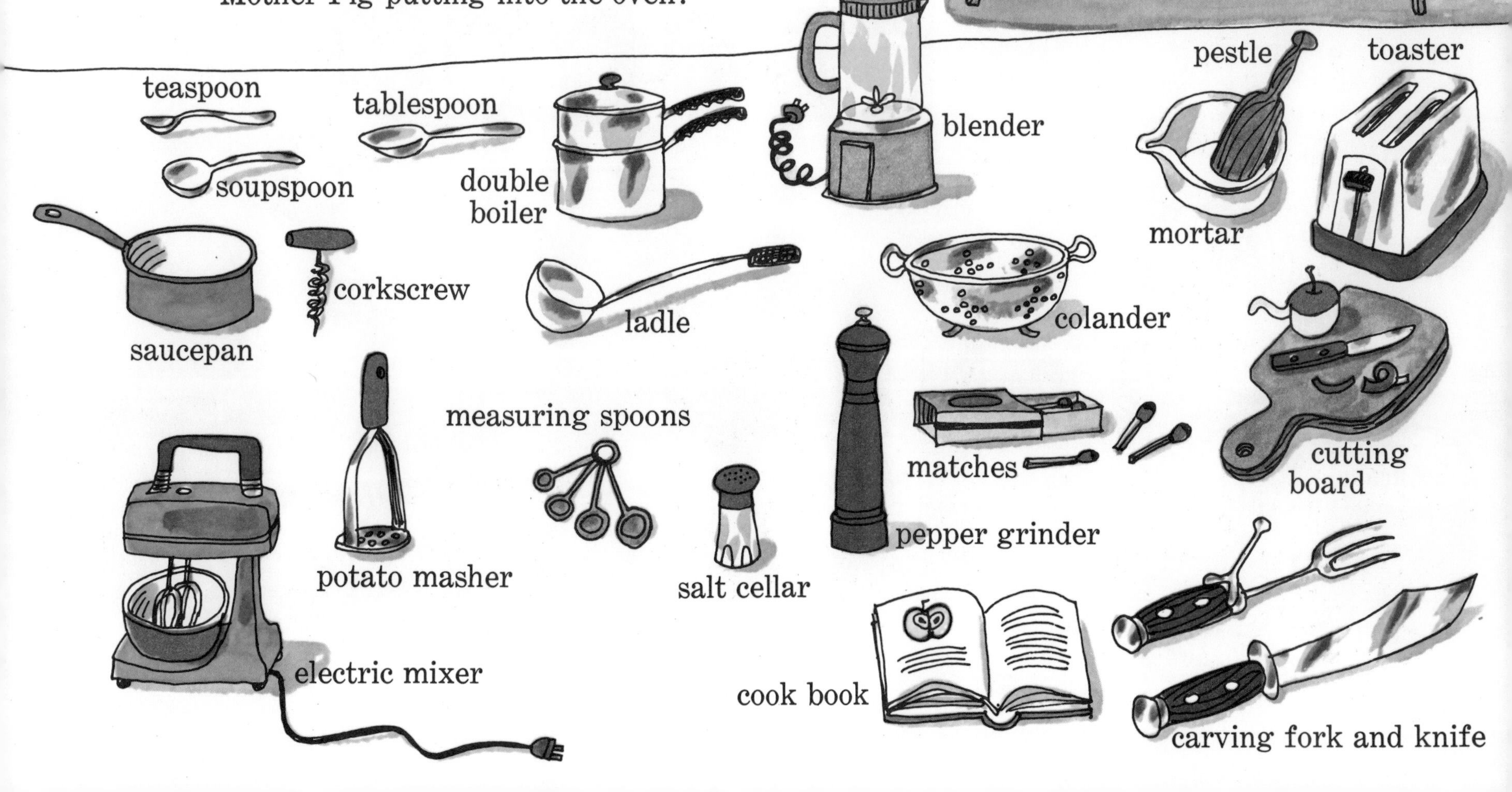

BUILDINGS

Buildings are used for different things. You wouldn't kick a ball in a museum or a cathedral. Where is a good place to kick a football? What do people do in the other buildings?

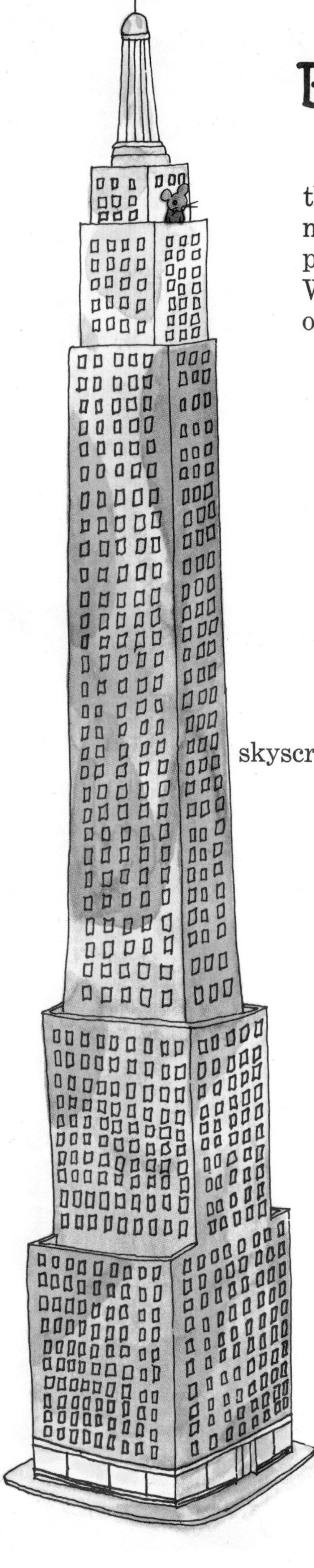

skyscraper

fort

tower

museum

arch

school

pyramid

football

stadium

windmill

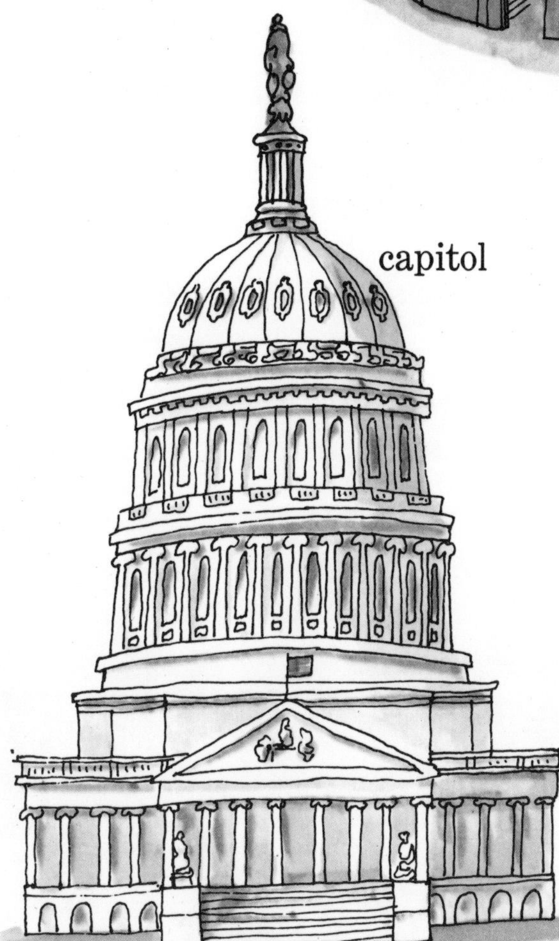

capitol

cathedral

church

library

factory

WHEN YOU GROW UP

What would you like to be when you are bigger? Would you like to be a good cook like your father? Or would you like to be a doctor or a nurse?

What would you like to be?

policeman

fireman

sailor

nurse

milkman

farmer

cowboy

doctor

carpenter

musician

butcher

dentist

secretary

good cook

singer
artist
pilot
fisherman
truck driver
teacher
garage mechanic
train conductor
commuter
store keeper
soldier
librarian
dancer
daddy
mommy

THE ALPHABET

The alligator is eating an apple.
The goose is wearing gloves.
What is the xiphias doing?

A alligator

B bear

C cat

D dog

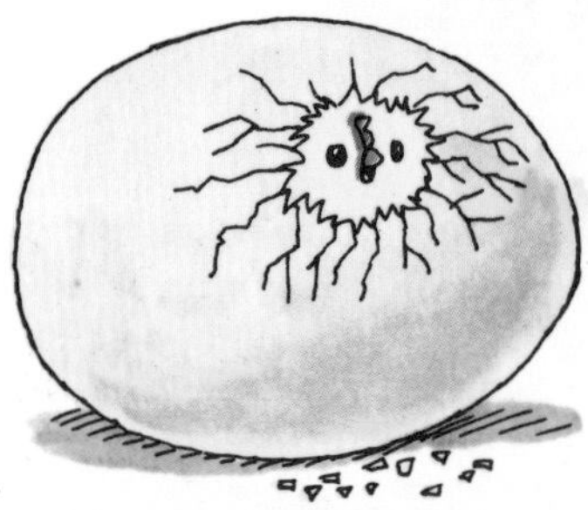

E egg

F fish

G goose

H heart

I ice cream

J Jack-o'-lantern

K kangaroo

L letter

M mailman

N nut

O owl

P present

Q queen

R rug

S spider

T turtle

U umbrella

V vase

W walrus

X xiphias

Y yarn

Z zipper

THINGS WE DO

There are many things
that we can do. And there
are some things we cannot do.
What is one thing we can't do?
Look and see.

dig

blow

build

break

sleep

awaken

walk

run

stand

sit

read

watch

draw and write

pull
push
kick
shout
talk
listen
whisper
eat
laugh
smile
cry
drink
jump over
crawl under
fall down
we can't fly
peek
tip a hat
go up
go down
go in
come out

WORK MACHINES

Busy, busy, busy bears. Most of the bears are busy moving dirt with their machines. But there is one bear who has a machine which does something else to the dirt. Which one is it? What is he doing?

tractor scraper
dump truck
tractor shovel
bucket loader
dirt
roller
smooth dirt
and tractor
rough dirt

automobile carrier
GASOLINE
A
milk truck
gasoline truck
sedan
motorcycle
tow truck
TAXI
TAXI
taxi
sports car

trailer truck

CARS AND TRUCKS

Down the street go the cars and trucks. But look! Some of the cars don't have drivers. Which cars have no drivers?

garbage truck

boat trailer

station wagon

motor scooter

antique car

school bus

HOTEL
GENERAL STORE
COWBOY SUITS
BOOTS
BANK
TOWN HALL
street lamp
hitching post
gold miner
burro
sheriff
cowboy
money box
frontier locomotive
headlight
BUFFALO BILL
stagecoach
wheel
cowcatcher

OUT WEST

Indian is coming to town to buy a horse for his squaw to ride. Why do you think it would be nice for her to have a horse to ride?

SHAPES AND SIZES

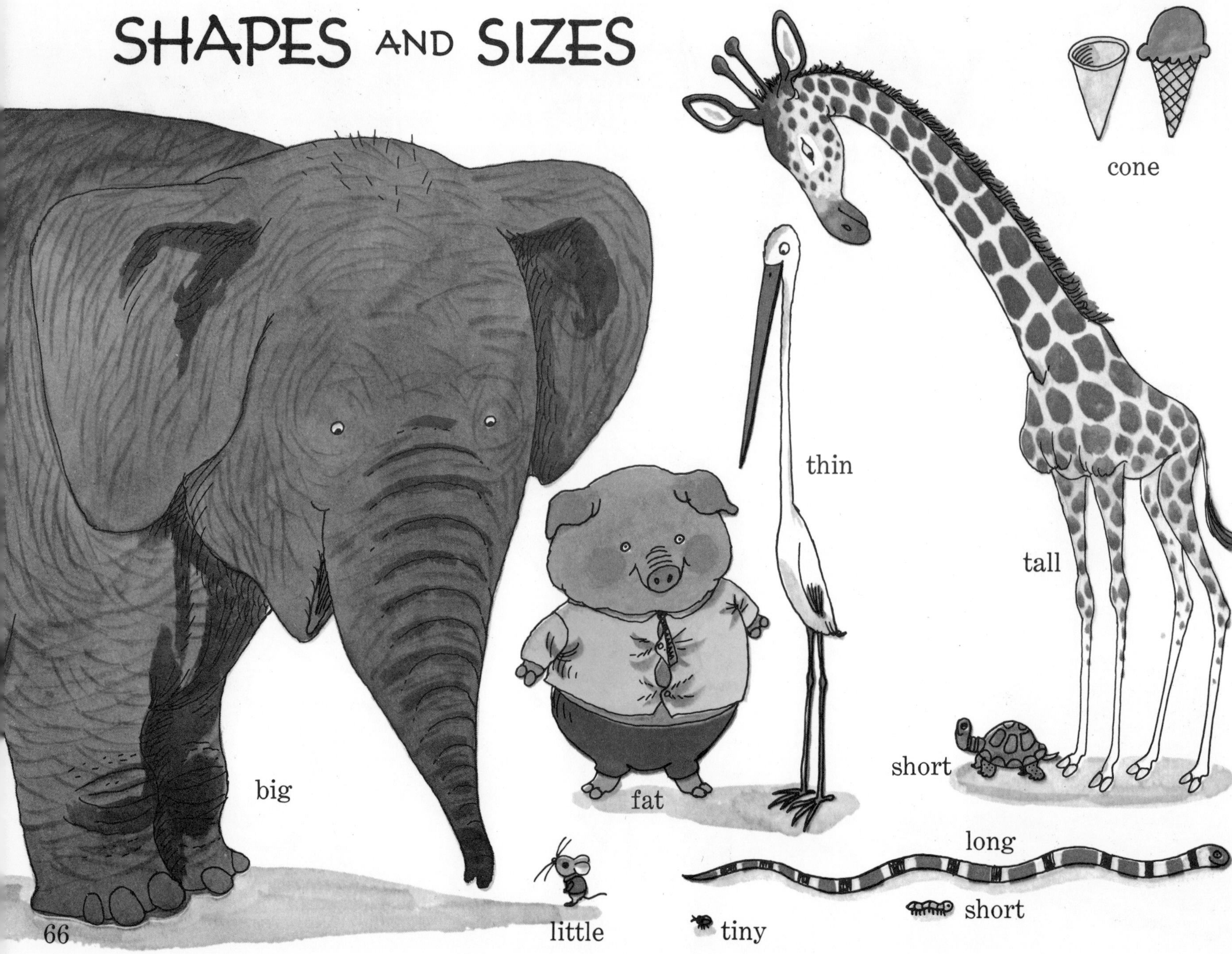

THE BABY

The cat family has a new baby kitten.
They don't know what to name it.
What would you like
to name the new baby?
Write the kitten's name here.

__ __ __ __ __ __

AT THE CIRCUS

The band is playing and the animals are doing their acts. What do you like to watch best at the circus?

pennant
circus tent
trapeze
trapeze artist
acrobat
safety net
ticket seller
hoop
lion
whip
juggler
cage
lion tamer
trained sea lion
balloon
man
popcorn man

THE FIREMEN TO THE RESCUE

Will the Brave Hero rescue the Beautiful Lady? I think he will. Don't you?

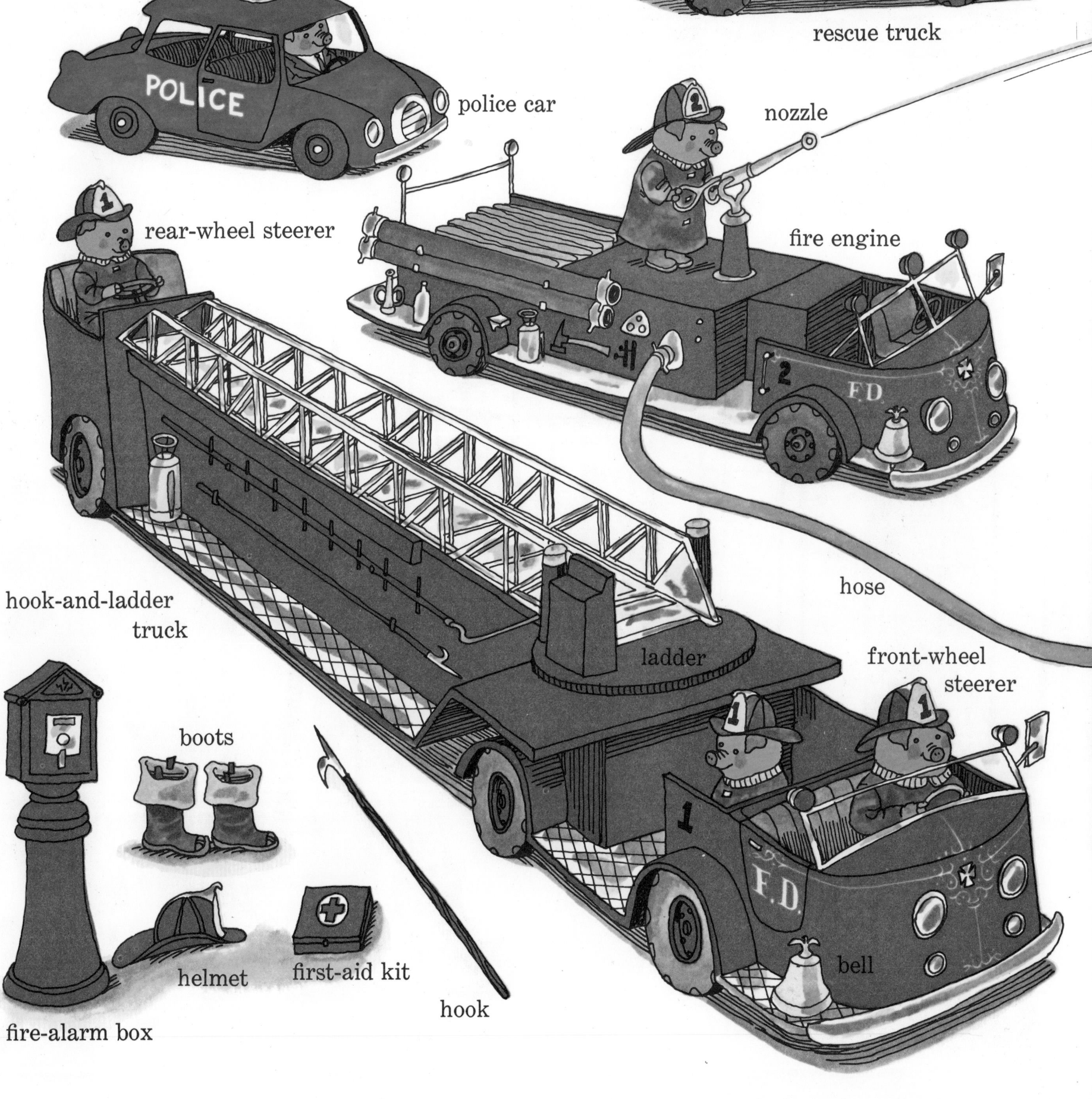

ambulance
F.D.
water
flames
smoke
fire chief
beautiful screaming lady
megaphone
CHIEF F.D.
fire chief's car
brave hero
pumper
F.D.
3
fire hydrant
jumping gentleman
ladder
firemen
rescue net
fireman
fire extinguisher

steam locomotive and tender

box car

TRAINS

Which train do you think
would be the most fun to run?
Would it be a freight train
or a passenger train?

hand car

caboose

flat car

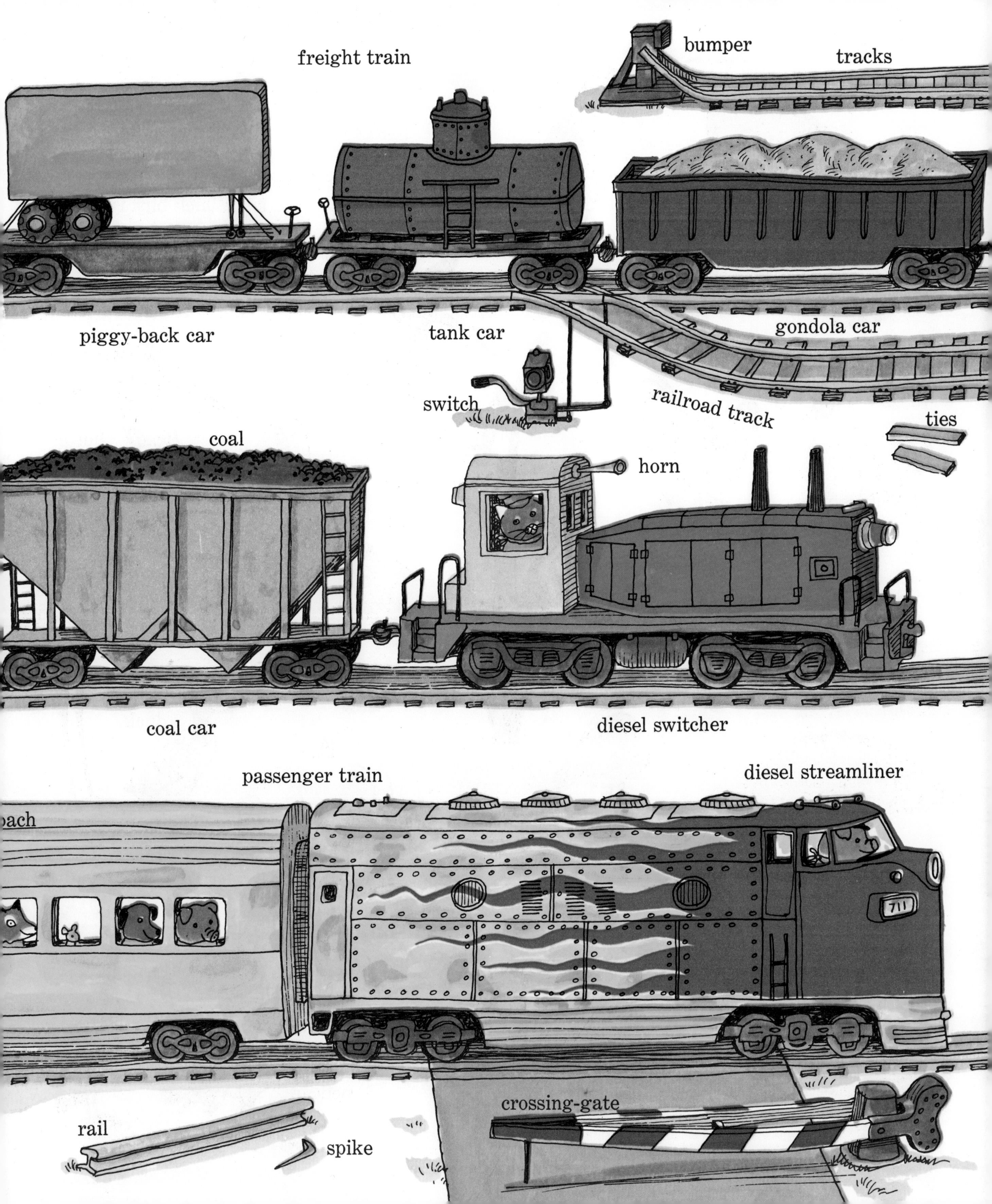
freight train
bumper
tracks
piggy-back car
tank car
gondola car
switch
railroad track
ties
coal
horn
coal car
diesel switcher
passenger train
diesel streamliner
711
crossing-gate
rail
spike

BIRDS

Most birds can fly. Some birds can't fly.
One bird who can't fly lives at the South Pole.
He likes to slide on the ice. Which bird is it?

vulture
parrot
crow
owl
toucan
ground dove
puffin
cardinal
bluejay
robin
bluebird
sparrow
wren
sea gull
sandpiper
tern
canary
bird house
bird cage
nest
baby birds
quail
pheasant
egret
stork
ostrich
woodcock
ostrich egg
starling

AT THE BEACH

In the summertime it is fun
to go to the beach.
What do you think
Rabbit hears in the seashell?
Is it the sound of the waves?

sea gull
umbrella
pavilion
sun
flag pole
sand dune
lifeguard
boardwalk
beach grass
stairs
bathhouse
beach chair
sea shell
starfish
sand fort
waves
shrimp
minnow
horseshoe crab
crab
flounder
seaweed
mussel

HOUSES

In different parts of the world people live in different kinds of houses. If you were invited to visit one of these houses, which would you like to stay in?

igloo

tree house

stone house

stilt house

mud hut

grass house

desert tent

wooden frame house

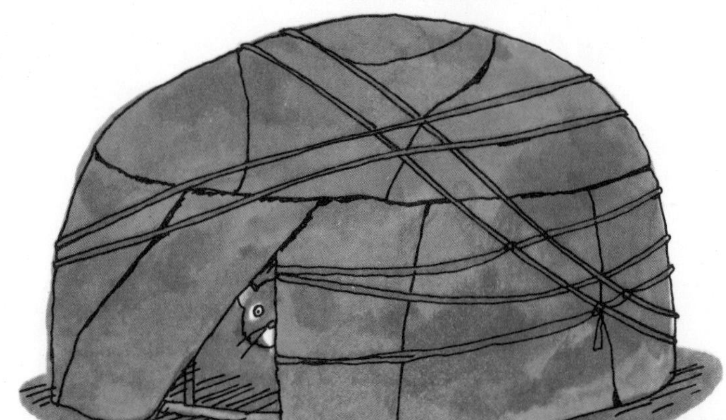

felt house

castle

half-timbered house

thatched-roof cottage

adobe house with tile roof

châlet

brick house

apartment house

houseboat

modern house

MAKING THINGS GROW

Everyone is working in the garden.
Mr. Crow has a seed in his mouth.
Do you think he will plant it?
Or will he eat it?

THE WEATHER

When we go outdoors we see what the weather is like. Sometimes it is sunny. Sometimes it is cloudy. It can be windy, or cold, or hot. It can be snowing or raining. What was the weather like outdoors today?

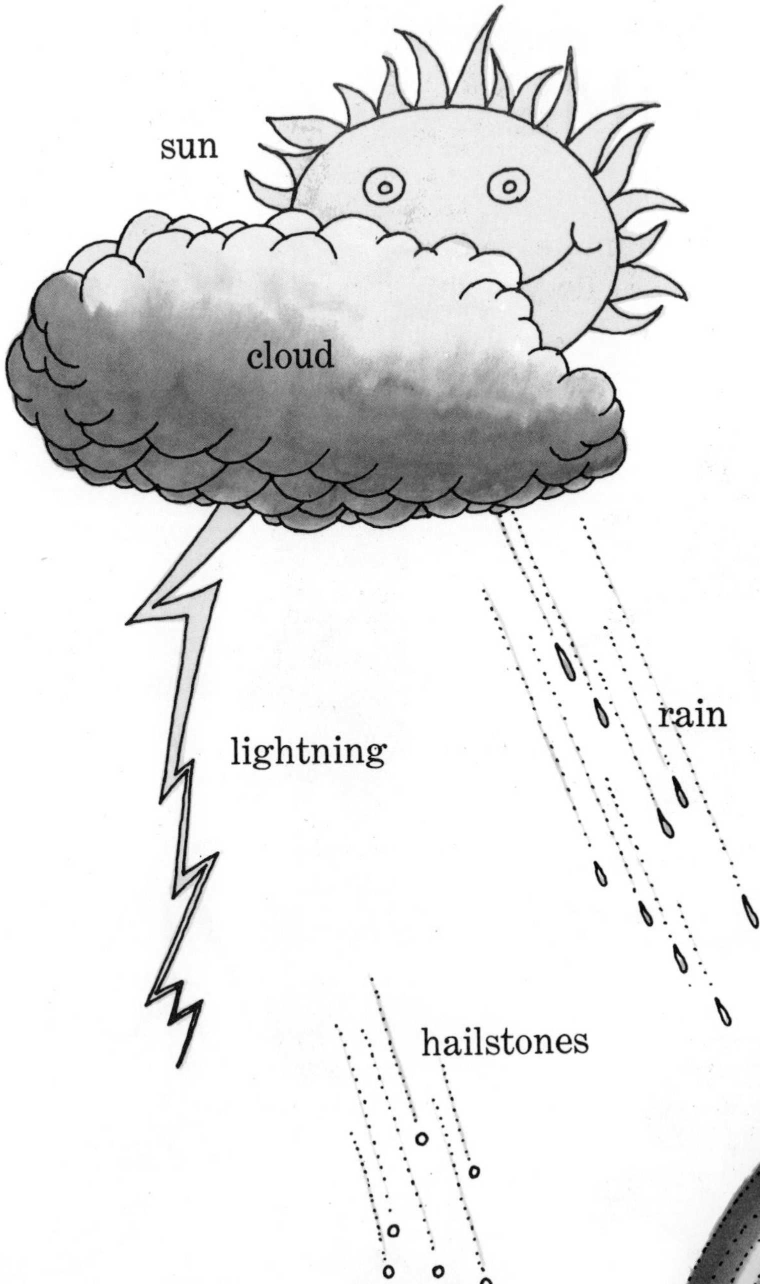

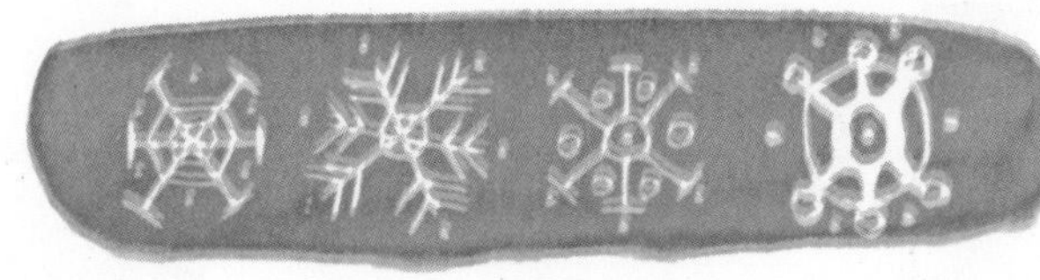

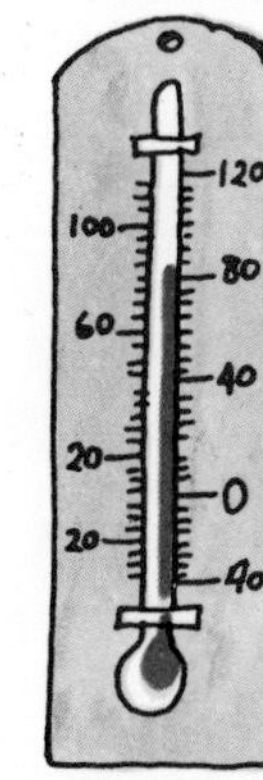

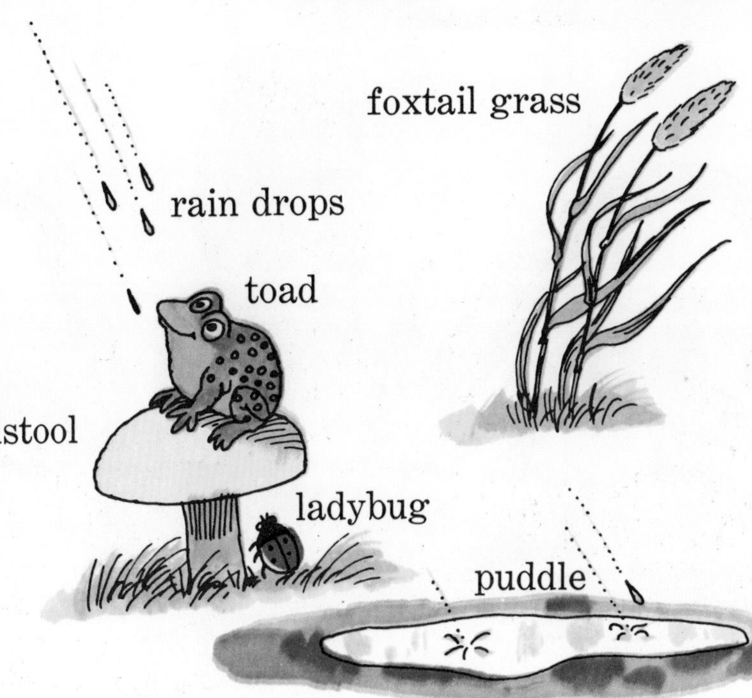

CLEAN-UP TIME

Each of the animals has a job to do to make everything tidy around the house. What do you think each animal is about to do?

muddy boots
footprints
chipped vase
chip
paw prints on the wall
closet pole
wire coat hanger
broken table leg
leaking faucet
brush
dust pan
wastebasket
fireplace ashes
bookcase
book
old newspapers
old magazines
wire coat hangers
Don't you think some of them
should be thrown in the ash can?
ash can or
garbage can

SPRING

Look at that baby lamb hop!
It is spring. He is happy.
Look at Mr. Bear coming out of
his cave! It is spring.
Now he can use his new
lawn mower.

SUMMER

Do you like to go
on picnics in the summertime?
Ants just love to go to picnics.
Do you know why?

FALL

In the Fall the air gets colder. The green leaves turn to bright colors. Then they fall to the ground. Is that why we say it is Fall at this time of year? Maybe it is.

WINTER

There are many ways to have fun on the snow and ice. Maybe you would like to do all of them. Would you?

LITTLE THINGS

Here are many little things.
What little thing do you sometimes
put on your Mommy's wall?

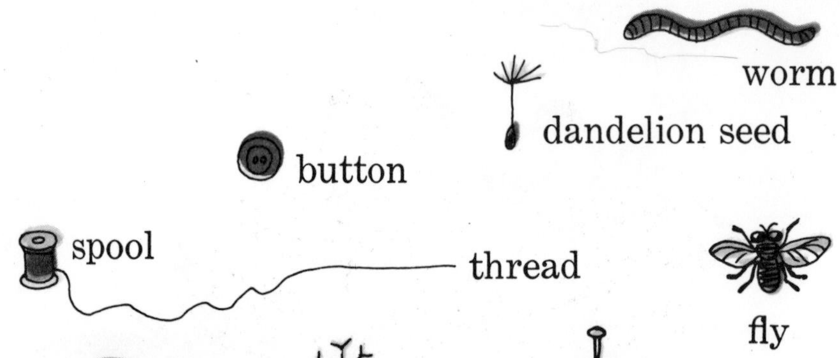

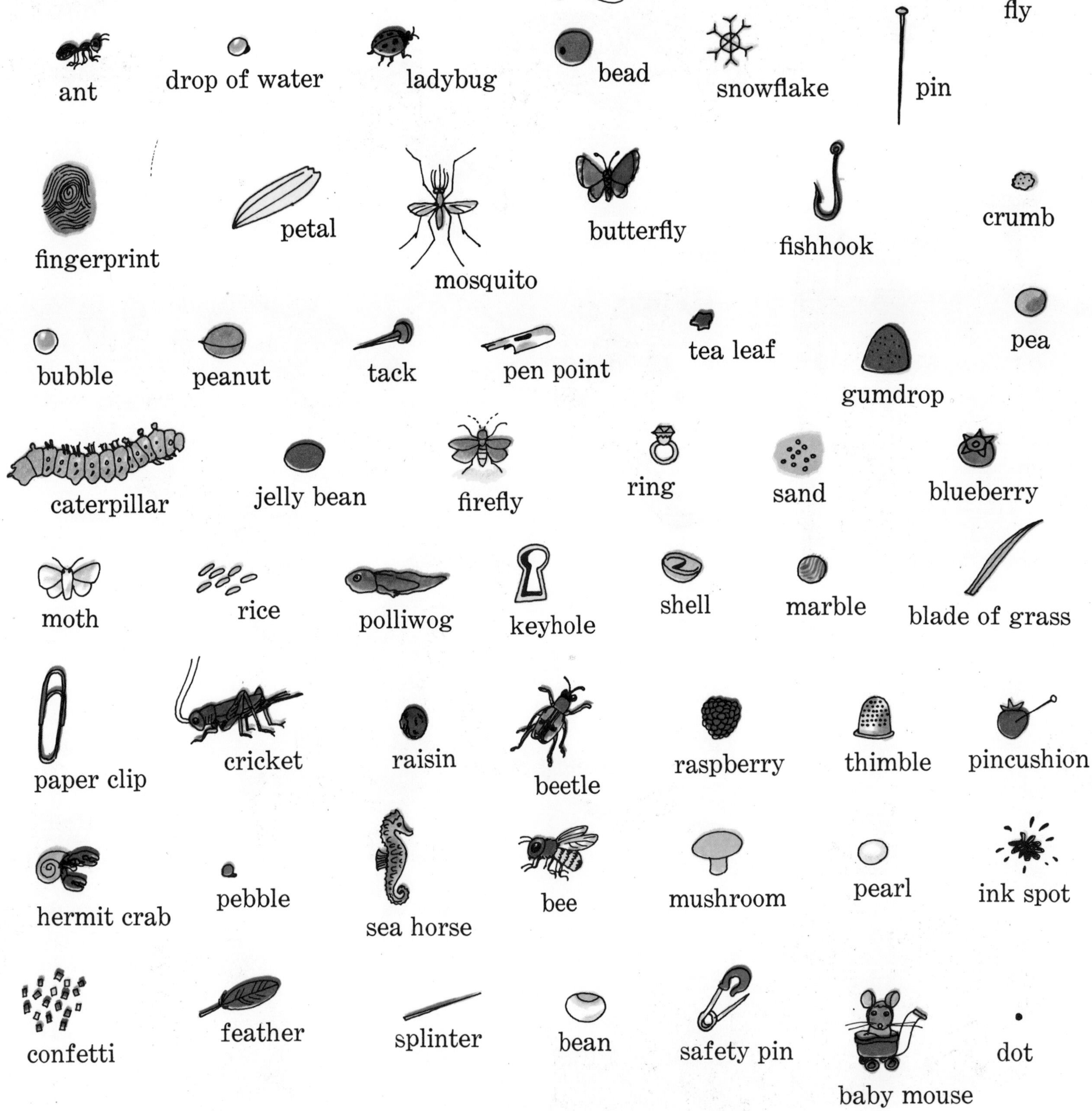

PARTS OF THE BODY

Bear picks things up in his paws.
What do you pick things up with?

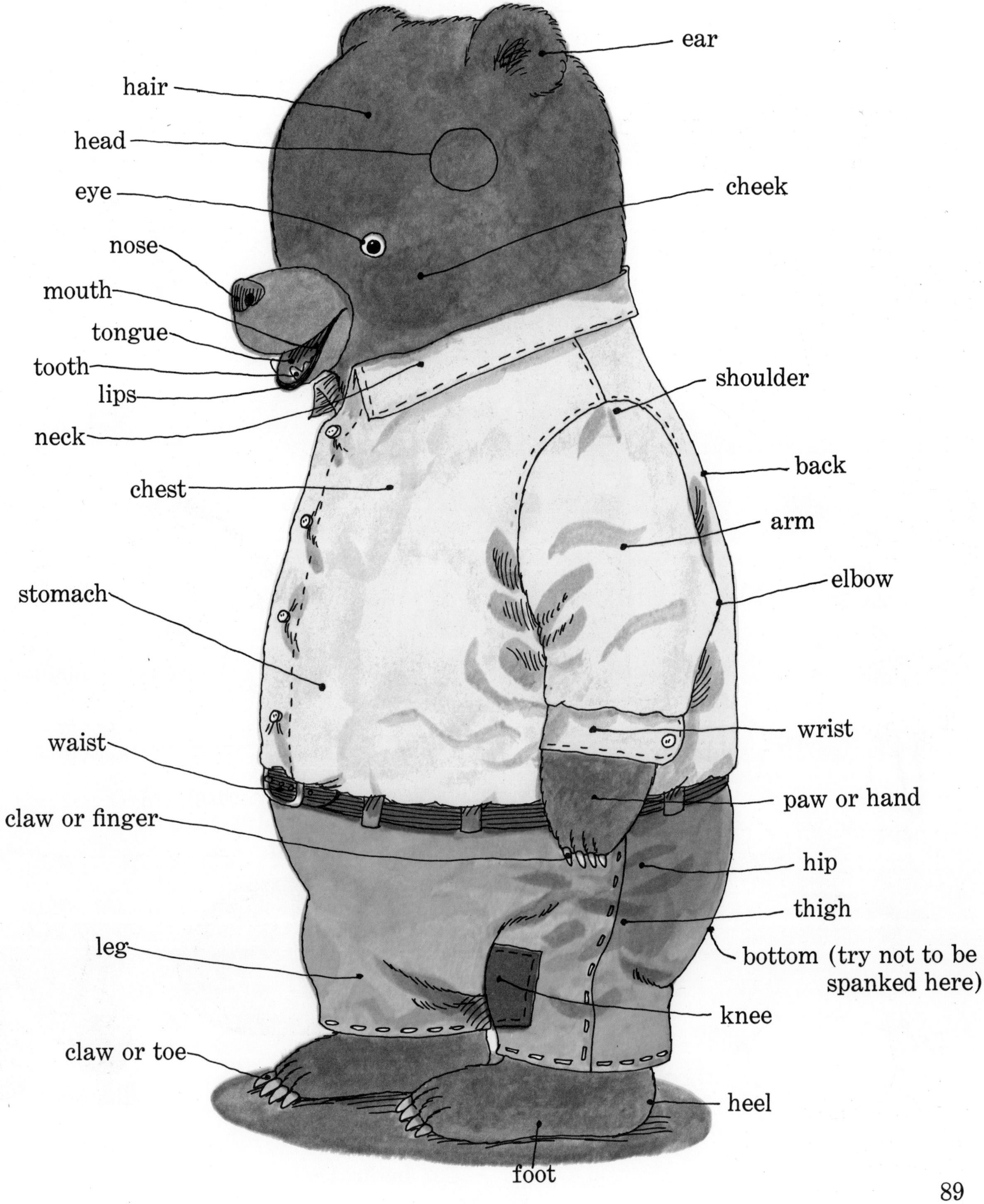

BEDTIME

Who is that hiding under the bed?
Find the naughty rascal and tell him to brush his teeth and get into bed.

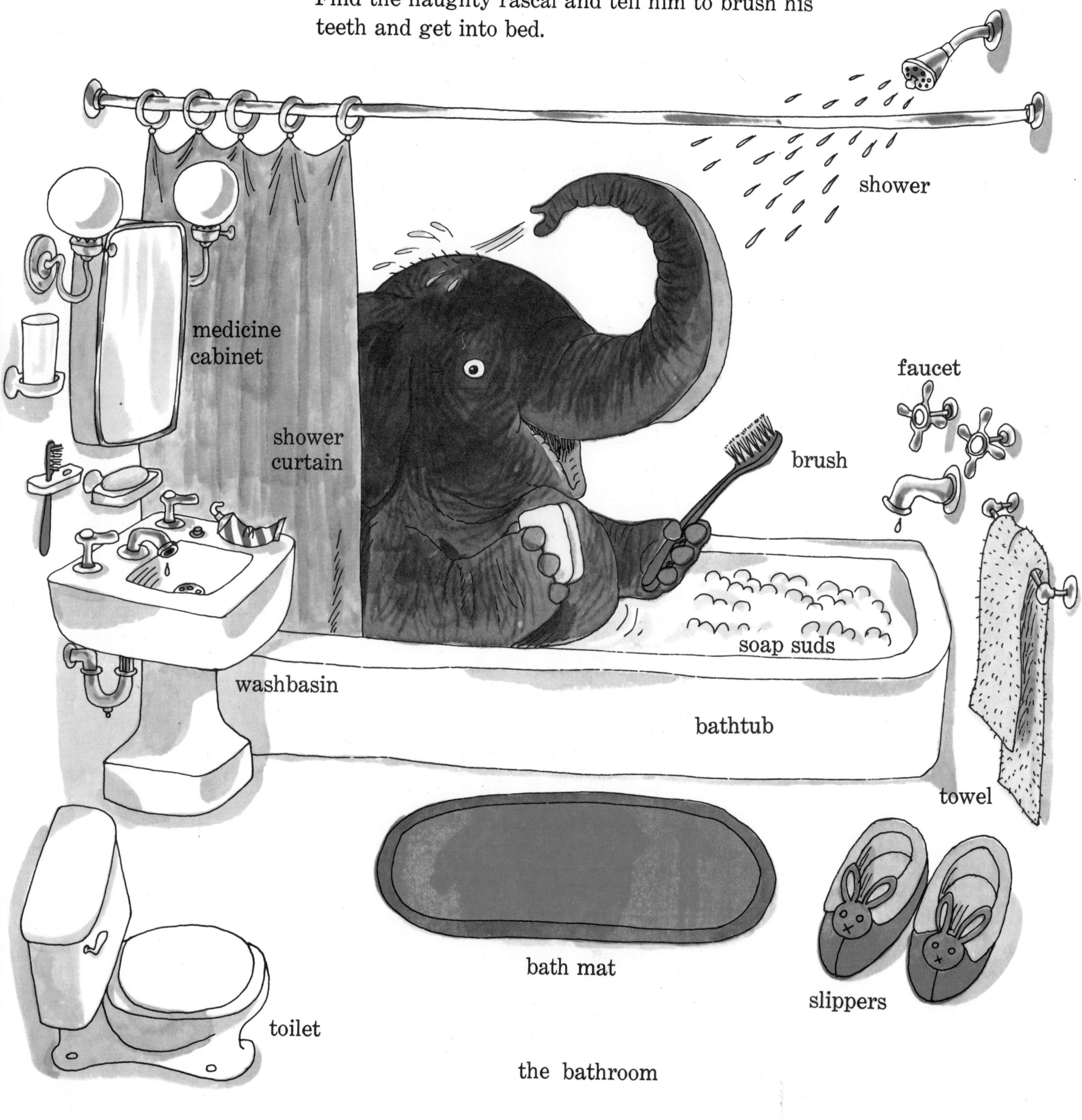

the bathroom

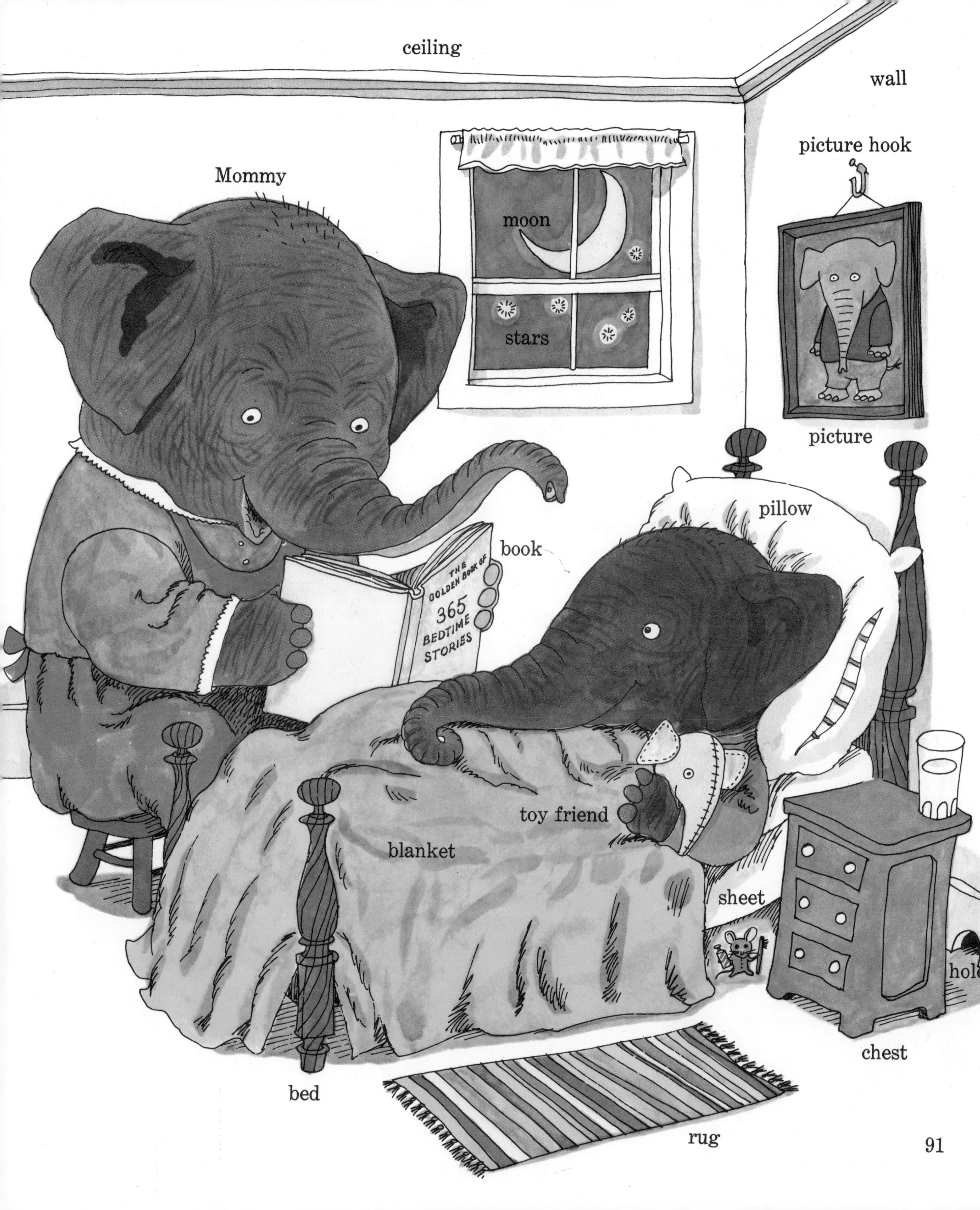
ceiling
wall
picture hook
Mommy
moon
stars
picture
pillow
book
THE GOLDEN BOOK OF 365 BEDTIME STORIES
toy friend
blanket
sheet
hole
chest
bed
rug

THE LAST WORDS OF THE DAY

The animals have a last word to say
before they go to bed.

Do you know what they are saying?
They are saying "Good night."

Walrus has some last words, too.
Do you know what he is saying?

rooster
hen
baby chick
mole
Sir Winston
London
England
letter
guitarist
crow
rabbit
spade
fly
pig
mouse
umbrella
vase
lamb
walrus